# *What the critics are saying...*

"A hilarious book that will have you chuckling throughout." ~ *Coffee Time Romance*

"Sexy and funny, OUT OF THIS WORLD is absolutely entertaining!" ~ *Romance Reviews Today.*

"What impressed me most about this story was Ms. Hardin's ability to make an intelligent, dare-I-say "geeky" hero sexy as sin." ~ *Just Erotic Romance Reviews*

D1711260

Ann Wesley Hardin

# OUT OF THIS WORLD

ELLORA'S CAVE
ROMANTICA PUBLISHING

An Ellora's Cave Romantica Publication

www.ellorascave.com

Out of This World

ISBN 9781419956218
ALL RIGHTS RESERVED.
Out of This World Copyright© 2006 Ann Wesley Hardin
Edited by Briana St. James
Cover art by Syneca

Electronic book Publication May 2006
Trade paperback Publication February 2007

Excerpt from *Riding Ranger* Copyright © Ciana Stone 2006

# Content Advisory:

## S – ENSUOUS
## E – ROTIC
## X – TREME

Ellora's Cave Publishing offers three levels of Romantica™ reading entertainment: S (S-ensuous), E (E-rotic), and X (X-treme).

The following material contains graphic sexual content meant for mature readers. This story has been rated E–rotic.

S-*ensuous* love scenes are explicit and leave nothing to the imagination.

E-*rotic* love scenes are explicit, leave nothing to the imagination, and are high in volume per the overall word count. E-rated titles might contain material that some readers find objectionable — in other words, almost anything goes, sexually. E-rated titles are the most graphic titles we carry in terms of both sexual language and descriptiveness in these works of literature.

X-*treme* titles differ from E-rated titles only in plot premise and storyline execution. Stories designated with the letter X tend to contain difficult or controversial subject matter not for the faint of heart.

# Also by Ann Wesley Hardin

ೋ

Coffee, Tea or Lea?

Layover

Miss Behavior


# About the Author

ೋ

They say there are eight million stories in the Naked City, and I think Jaci Burton wrote every single one of them. I don't know. She must've sneezed and missed a deadline because here I am at Ellora's Cave, and I couldn't be more thrilled.

Addicted to love? You bet. As well as all its sensual side effects. Great sex comes in many packages and I prefer mine wrapped in laughter, irony and sweet, edible substances. When not writing at the computer, I can be found in a fencing salle, cruising Internet auctions for vintage airline memorabilia, yelling at my children to let mommy write, or working my schleppy nine-to-fiver. When I grow up, I'd like to be a full time Ellora's Cave writer, but until then, I'll just frolic in the outskirts of the Naked City.

Bon Voyage!

Ann welcomes comments from readers. You can find her website and email address on her author bio page at www.ellorascave.com.

# OUT OF THIS WORLD

 හ

# Dedication

❦

*For Bree, for loving this story as much as I do and for stretching my skills way beyond what I thought I could do. In fact, I now have stretch marks.*

*And for Dana, who would marry Arnie if he existed, and who gives me Moppits whenever I sell a manuscript.*

*It's nice to be spongeworthy.*

# Trademarks Acknowledgement

The author acknowledges the trademarked status and trademark owners of the following wordmarks mentioned in this work of fiction:

BMW: Bayerische Moteren Werke Aktiengesellschaft Corporation

Casper the Friendly Ghost: Harvey Entertainment, Inc.

Cessna: Cessna Aircraft Company

Chrysler: Daimler Chrysler Corporation

Disney World: Disney Enterprises, Inc.

John Deere: Deere & Company

MENSA: American Mensa, Ltd.

Mooney: Aerostar Aircraft Corporation of Texas

Porsche: Porsche Aktiengesellschaft Corporation

Ray-Ban: Luxottica S.r.l. LTD LIAB

Sky-Watcher: Pacific Telescope Corp.

Spam: Hormel Food, LLC LTD LIAB Co.

# PROLOGUE

**Memorandum: The Directive—TestFate**
**StarDate: 10,015**
**From: Queen Win**
**To: Probabilist Anthros**

Good work on the biology, culture and belief system of the Earthling humanoids. Now I would like to test this theory of the concept they call "Fate", especially as it pertains to mating. Too many of them believe in it to dismiss it as the byproduct of overactive imaginations.

To test this theory, I would like two like-minded infants from our breeding stock to be planted on Earth as far apart as possible. I want them raised as humans. Be sure to monitor them closely during any and all mating rituals. Let the essence of sexuality be your guide, as it normally is.

Being from our world, these plants will be genetically wired to receive our signals and might sense your presence if they're open to it, just as the Earthlings sometimes do. This cannot be helped. However, I command you to maintain as low a profile as possible. Do not frighten them, but rather maintain a benign demeanor throughout their lifecycle. In this way they might get used to you and think nothing of it.

Above all, do not interfere—unless there is danger of one mating with a human. If this happens, alert me and we will stage an intervention.

According to the human laws of fate, our two infants should meet and "fall in love". When and if this occurs, we will decide how to proceed.

# CHAPTER ONE

The unmistakable thunk of an unbalanced airplane propeller overhead didn't sit well with Arnie Simpson as he diddled under the hood of his Porsche.

He had no need to peel his eyes from the pistons to recognize Tom Littleton's Cessna, despite the troubling racket. He knew every aircraft in the region, who owned it and how it should sound on final approach.

"Genius Chrysler!" Arnie slammed the hood of the classic speedster, jammed the keys into the ignition, and took off down the dirt road to Flintlock Municipal Airport.

While he drove, he kept one eye on the plane—not that that would prevent it from tumbling out of the sky like Dorothy's house in *The Wizard of Oz*—but it seemed the right thing to do.

A hundred yards out and about to radio the firehouse, he realized Tom would make it. Barely.

Arnie let out a breath he didn't know he'd been holding, tucked the Porsche into a parking spot and jogged to the runway.

Tom clunked safely in.

"Bring her over here." Arnie semaphored the feverish plane to a scrap of shade on the tarmac. He trotted inside the hangar for his mechanic's tools and began combing over the engine.

"Saw you hop in your race car and had a feeling it was worse than I thought," Tom said, climbing out of the plane and ambling over with a grin.

Arnie didn't maintain a MENSA membership to suffer fools gladly. Particularly pilots moronic enough to overlook a notch in the prop during a preflight inspection. The forces at work had turned the notch into a fracture and Tom's prop had a chunk bitten out the size of a ping-pong ball. His engine was on the verge of breaking up from the strain. The nitwit was too lucky for his own knickers. "I suggest you go buy me some prop wash," Arnie said when Tom showed signs of settling in for a jaw. Prop wash didn't exist. Should keep the pinhead out of his hair.

"Sure thing." Tom trotted off.

While Arnie worked up a mental and physical lather under the ailing Cessna's nose, he pondered the human intellect, or lack thereof, and the existence of superior life forms. Or lack thereof.

It would be sweet, he thought, to talk to creatures who understood what he said. Too bad they were too few and too far in between.

His amateur cohorts at the E.T. Institute—where they listened for missives from the cosmos—made for some pretty entertaining company, most of the time. But they were too geeky for words. Arnie had his feet firmly planted in both worlds. And found both to be ultimately lonely.

He'd had a great life, had been happy during most of it. The parents had given him a decent childhood, when they'd had the time. How their genes ever lined up to produce him was another story.

He had no idea why he'd been picked out of the passel to carry the brain load. Just some freak of nature, some quasi-funny joke played by the gods by tucking him in the middle of a family whose combined IQs were about half of his.

If that.

He loved them. Fiercely. But that didn't stop him from realizing they were dodo birds. What if he carried dimwit genes and passed them down to his kids? How would he cope? Mating with another species from outer space would certainly abolish that risk.

The discovery of other life in the universe had been a lifelong fantasy of his, but more than that, it'd been a lifelong *craving*. There simply had to be more out there. More intelligence, more weird people like him. Otherwise, his existence really would be a joke. And not a very funny one at that.

He wondered what it would be like when aliens finally made irrefutable contact. What the circumstances would be. How would the public react? There'd been some promising signals bleeping through the E.T. Institute's scanners the last few years, leading Arnie, his friends and other experts to believe they were on the cusp of a breakthrough. Many had concluded aliens were already here, and had been for years. Although Arnie wasn't so sure, occasionally he met someone who made him believe. But that hadn't happened in a while. Come to think of it, he hadn't gotten that hair-raising feeling of being watched lately, either. Maybe he'd finally reached a plateau of normalcy in his life, after all.

Right. As if that would ever happen.

Leaning back for a break from his work and his musings, he heard the familiar drone of Gage Archer's Mooney lining up with the runway.

Gage had been back and forth to Minneapolis all week, ferrying his fiancée's family in for their upcoming wedding. Since Arnie was best man, he wondered idly who today's passenger would be and he watched as the air taxi greased the concrete and hummed to a spot nearby.

What he saw emerging from the door made his mouth dry up.

It was a woman.

That in itself wasn't usually enough to drain the spit out of Arnie's mouth. Hell, he saw women every day of his life.

This one was incredibly…odd-looking.

Arnie never paid much attention to anyone's appearance, male or female. He cared less about what was shown than what was hidden—namely brains, or lack thereof.

But that hair.

It was white.

Not platinum blonde, or fake in any way—but downright, unmistakably, white. What's more, it looked soft. And long as a Martian winter.

She had an unusual aura surrounding her that he could plainly see. It seemed to undulate, and vibrate. Were those her emotions? Her thoughts?

Whatever the visible energy emanating from her was, it was doing outlandish things to his dick. Things no other woman had ever done at first sight.

He couldn't comprehend his body's fascination with this woman and he suddenly harbored some serious doubts that someone so instantly alluring could possibly be an Earthling. He didn't even know her IQ! Had Gage's plane taken a detour to Andromeda? Stranger things had happened according to the E.T. Institute. And wasn't a visitation not only possible but probable and imminent?

Her figure was slender and supple, with average-sized breasts jutting out from her pale green T-shirt. In that regard she appeared humanoid enough.

She was in terrific shape for her age—looked thirty when she had to be fifty, assuming she'd been spawned on this planet.

But fuck if he cared how many years she had under her belt or which nebula she blew in from. Those small details just didn't matter to Arnie. Brains were what interested him and now, white hair.

* * * * *

Dr. Ava Ward grabbed her shoulder bag off the floor of the Mooney and paused to make sure nothing had tumbled out.

"Ready to go?" Gage asked from behind.

"Aye, aye, Captain," she grinned, spinning around and firing off a stiff, crisp salute.

He rolled his eyes and smiled. "Just give me a second to lock up."

"The flight was a blast, thanks!"

"Service is my motto."

Ava looked around with excitement. Gage had been a sensational tour guide, buzzing cow fields, pointing out Wisconsin's places of interest and making the flight a helluva lot of fun. And Flintlock had looked kind of cool from the air. What there was of it, anyway.

Most of the time Ava didn't take to small towns. Found the people either too nosy or too standoffish. There seemed to be no in betweens. And she would know. She'd been born and raised in Fairbanks, Alaska, and that was smaller than she could stand.

She'd come to Flintlock for two reasons, to stand as Lorna's maid of honor and try to have a hot hook-up with the best man. Lorna had been gabbing about him incessantly, insisting he and Ava were soul mates and that the requisite happily-ever-after would be apparent with one glance.

Ava wasn't buying it. From Lorna's description he seemed uncannily intelligent but unwilling to use that intelligence for any worthwhile pursuits. If there was one thing she would never tolerate in a man, it was laziness. Her father had been well intentioned and loving, but lazy. He had died broke, leaving her and her mother to fend for themselves. That was no way to treat your family. So the jury was still out on forever with Arnie Simpson. But a wedding fling was eminently doable.

After all, wasn't that what normal, red-blooded single girls were supposed to do at weddings? Not that she'd ever been considered normal, or that when push came to shove she actually wanted to *be* normal. But she did want to fit in with the crowd for once in her life. This was a vacation. Her first in years. And she planned on living it to the hilt.

Her best friend was going to help. "Too bad Lorna couldn't come with you to pick me up." Gage had been in such a rush at Dane County Airport, and the ride had been so noisy, Ava'd barely had a chance to ask about her.

"Deadline," Gage said. "Had time to throw a hissy fit about it though."

Ava laughed. Back home in Minneapolis Lorna was known as Miss Behavior, the etiquette expert. Her newspaper column was an enormous success. So much so that she'd been able to write her own ticket. A one-way ticket to Flintlock to marry Gage.

"She's been having problems setting up the home office and getting online," Gage added as he bent to put chocks behind the Mooney's wheels. "Flintlock isn't known for having multiple providers."

"I bet," Ava grimaced. So far, Lorna hadn't had to commute back to Minneapolis too often, but when she did, Gage was right there to ferry her.

Ava sighed. Lorna had found the true love they'd always craved, while Ava was still stuck in an office with her fingers up old men's asses.

Ah well, it was a living.

"Let's go." Gage snagged her duffel.

Turning to follow him inside the small airport, she froze dead in her tracks. A man wearing an oily AirGage T-shirt, torn jeans and buckskin steel toes leaned against a neighboring airplane. With one elbow buttressing the fuselage and both hands fiddling with a pipe wrench, he struck a swoon-worthy pose—gawking at Ava as if she'd just beamed down from a spaceship.

Since her unusual coloring often elicited such a reaction, she didn't take offense. She simply stood transfixed, gawking right back. "He work for you?" she asked Gage sotto voce, staring at some totally astounding pecs.

"What? Oh. That's Arnie. My mechanic."

Ava's jaw dropped another notch. *That's Arnie Simpson? The best man. Hubbariffic!*

There he stood, the man who had such awesome genius he was constantly hounded with job offers from NASA—and constantly blowing them off. According to Lorna, he'd gotten stellar scores on every aptitude test known to mankind, attended MIT on full scholarship and yet he preferred to rot right here in Flintlock fixing crop dusters.

Apparently, you could take the man out of the country but not the country out of the man. The seventh of ten offspring of Wisconsin hog farmers, he held the seeds of greatness in his hands but had yet to sow them.

Still, he had brains. And beauty. Two-thirds of what she required in a mate, making him better suited to her than most.

*Except…*

She batted the soul mate carrot away from her nose. If she could rustle him out of the stockyards and into Mission Control where he belonged, she'd take a big, juicy bite. Until then he was purely fun in the sun. Nothing more.

If looks were anything to go on, what fun it could be.

"Hey, Arnie," Gage said. "Suck the drool back in your mouth and get over here. There's someone I want you to meet."

Blast! She hadn't checked her lipstick before landing. Now she'd look like Casper the Friendly Ghost.

In slow motion, Arnie set down his tool and pushed away from the plane. He advanced with measured steps, as if unsure of himself. Ava didn't like that. Confidence turned her on. His wariness gave her a sharper edge than she'd had a minute ago, when she'd felt the lick of his eyes against her skin.

The closer he got, the duller her edge grew. He had that sexy economy of movement only shorter men possessed. Her top teeth clamped down to chew some life into her lips and she saw him falter for a second.

His body, compact and muscular, had perfect athletic proportions. On top of that, he had a sun-bronzed brown mop of hair that cried out for a tango with feminine fingers.

Longish sideburns framed his way-cute face in the manner of a beatnik. All he needed was a black mock turtleneck, pencil pants and loafers and he could slide right into a Sixties' Parisian jazz club.

He stopped beside her, creeping into her personal space even though he stood a good four feet away. Ava slipped her brown Ray Bans with the bottle green lenses over her hair like a headband and extended a perfectly manicured hand. Well, almost perfect. The clipped nails were a concession to her profession.

"Best Man Arnie, meet Maid of Honor Ava." Gage said in a voice tinged with amusement.

She met his eyes as Gage made the introductions and found herself absorbed by scrumptious color. Deep brown with amber flecks, as if someone had sprinkled gold dust into a fondue pot of dark chocolate.

What, oh what would those large round eyes look like suspended above her, heavy with passion and need?

Her pussy got damp.

* * * * *

"Pleasure," Arnie said, wiping his hand on his ass and shaking hers.

He tried to stare at her left ear, half afraid of what he might find in her eyes. But like a dope, he overshot and his gaze hit hers. Bull's-eye.

Green. That figured. The eyes were alien green to match all that Milky Way hair.

Crapola.

This was bad.

Scanning her face, his knees nearly buckled when he realized her satiny, succulent skin was as tensile as a trampoline, putting her well under fifty in people years.

He wanted to bounce all over her.

Did that hair color even exist in this galaxy? He noticed her brows and lashes were darker, almost smoky. They intrigued him enough to wonder what color the hair down under might be. And make him itch to find out. Soon.

Even if she was thick as a plank, dull as a dormouse, Arnie figured he'd have to investigate every inch of that pert, long-limbed body. After all, it was his duty to the legacy of Hangar Eighteen.

Before he could stop himself from a move so atypically bold even Gage drew back in surprise, he reached up and captured a few strands of that hair in his fingers, twirling them gently into a double helix.

"All the women in my family go white early," Ava said, smiling. "I've had this color since med school."

Arnie blinked and dropped his hand. "You're a doctor?" *Sent down to perform experiments?*

She couldn't be for real. There simply had to be something wrong with her. Maybe she'd gotten her degree from the back of a magazine or from some whacked-out third-world country. *Or Venus.*

"Yeah. Harvard class of '97."

Crap.

"That so?" Arnie asked to hide his increasing fear. "I graduated MIT in '95."

"We just missed each other," Ava laughed.

"Imagine that," he muttered and for the life of him, couldn't think of another thing to say except a silent *Halleluiah* she hadn't been orbiting Massachusetts during final exams. Not that he needed to study or anything, he wasn't that lame, but she might've been a bit of a distraction—because of the white hair, of course.

"Listen," Gage said with a pointed glance at his watch. "I'd love to stand around discussing microphysics with you brainiacs all day, but Lorna is expecting us."

"I hate small talk," Ava quipped.

She and Arnie giggled like two nutty kids.

Because he wondered if anything living would shift inside when he lifted it, he bent down to retrieve Ava's luggage. Nope, no specimens that he could feel.

Yet.

He fell into line behind Gage as they headed to his taxicab.

\* \* \* \* \*

Ava brought up the rear, studying Arnie's assets with more than professional interest. Oh to have him bending *her* over on the examining table—armed with a French tickler and strawberry-flavored body lotion. Not something she'd ever had the opportunity to try. But there was still time.

"Here we go," Gage said.

"Nice cab." She ran a hand along a sleek, black fender. He'd imported a London taxicab as part of his complete livery service. She had to admire his initiative. Lorna said he had a corner on the transportation market in Flintlock and just about every borough all the way into Madison. A small-town magnate had captured the heart of her big-city friend.

That would never happen to Ava. No way would she ever live in Podunk again, even if it did give birth to a pocket-rocket scientist. Her gaze slid over Arnie once more.

With a breathtaking ripple of biceps, he hiked her bag into the trunk, slammed it and stepped over to open the passenger door.

"I suggest it's been a pleasure."

Ava suddenly wondered how it would be to see him smile. At her. Bet you have an awesome grin, she told him silently. "Nice meeting you too, Arnie. Guess I'll see you at the rehearsal."

"If not before." Gage smirked.

Arnie ducked his head, and, as if receiving her silent request, his lips parted over straight glistening teeth. A pleasure shock undulated through her body, turning her thoughts to the wedding night and a consummation with him. On a baby grand. With…handcuffs.

"Got a load of work to do on the Cessna." He backed away slowly, dark gaze slipping around hers and igniting the pheromone fumes between them. "See you at the Hangaround later?"

"Yup," Gage said, sliding behind the wheel.

With a small, regretful wave, Ava followed suit. At the last minute, Arnie lunged forward and closed the door for her. Rapping the roof with his knuckles in goodbye, he turned on his heel and jogged back to the hangar.

Ava had to remember to blink once he rounded the corner. His looks had her pussy throbbing and his manners had her heart aching. How long had it been since a man opened and closed a door for her? She couldn't remember. Most of the time, people let the door slam behind them, never looking to see who might be following. And forget about getting a thank you for holding a door. Ava's thoughts stalled. Arnie hadn't gotten one from her either.

That realization disappointed her.

"What's the Hangaround?" she asked in an attempt to gloss over sudden remorse.

"Airport bar and grill. We eat there once in a while."

"Arnie's going tonight?" Maybe she'd get a chance to be polite. And more.

"He's there every night."

Sounded like no girlfriend in the picture then. She'd have to quiz Lorna to make sure.

Six minutes later they arrived at the homestead. "Ava!" Lorna flew out the door when Gage honked the horn.

Before Ava could find the latch, Lorna was there, yanking the cab door open, and hauling her out over the curb into a tight embrace. Where had her restrained, excruciatingly polite friend gone?

"Welcome to the monkey house," Gage said.

"How was the flight? Did you get sick? Did you and Gage have any problems finding each other? How are you?"

"Everything went fine," Ava said, smiling. It was fantastic to see Lorna again. The last time they'd met in Minneapolis, she'd been so busy arranging things at the newspaper and planning her wedding they'd hardly had time to catch up.

Lorna hooked arms with her while Gage shouldered her suitcase. When he'd slammed the trunk lid, they ambled up the small, neat walkway to the small, not-so-neat house.

"Isn't it great?" Lorna gushed. "Finally. My own home."

"Unreal!" Ava hedged. Yick. That's what love did to a person.

"C'mon, I'll show you the guestroom."

They squeezed down a short, narrow hallway to one of the two bedrooms.

*Feng shui's got nothing on Lorna.* Ava surveyed the tiny room. White, bright and bare. A double bed with a brushed aluminum hospital-style headboard took up most of one wall. A battered dresser filled the other. Across the smattering of visible wood flooring lay a prim swath of coir.

"Incredible," Ava breathed.

"Put her suitcase on the floor, for now," Lorna instructed Gage.

Ava wondered where Lorna intended putting it later.

"Guess I'll head back to the airport to help Arnie," Gage said with a jingle of keys. "Leave you to your girl talk." He gave Ava's hair an affectionate ruffle. "Glad you're here."

Once he left, Lorna hustled Ava into the kitchen. Like the old days, she had a pot of tea already prepared. Sliding two steaming cups onto the table, she pulled out a chair for Ava and sat herself down on the other side. "Well, what did you think of Arnie?"

Ava stirred a teaspoon of sugar into her tea, tapped the spoon and set it on a napkin. "He's not what I expected."

"What?"

She grinned. "You didn't tell me he was so hot."

Lorna slumped in relief. "Like you'd have believed me. I mean. Come on! Beauty *and* brains?"

*And Hot Grease-Monkey Sex stamped on his ass.* "True. True." Arnie had it all. Except a city address and family-sized wages. More the better, actually, she reminded herself. Would make it easier to say goodbye after the hot sex.

"Any vibes from him?"

Ava winked. "Besides the fact he couldn't take his eyes off my body?"

Lorna whooped, hopping up and scooping Ava into another excited hug. "I did it. I did it."

"Calm down. We don't even know each other."

"Yes, you do. In here." Lorna tapped over her heart with a forefinger. "Besides, I know you both and I say since you're both attracted, it's a done deal."

Ava had to laugh. They were attracted all right but she knew better than to pin too many hopes on that alone. "There're several major hurdles. Including my job." *And this town, and Arnie's lack of ambition.*

"Well, you just won't tell him."

Ava sat back down and ran a hand through her hair. "Of course I'll tell him."

"No. You won't." Lorna set her chin.

"I have to."

Lorna crossed her arms over her chest and leaned against the kitchen counter as if settling in for a fight. "No. You don't."

For a smart woman, Lorna could be pretty thick sometimes. Ava waved a hand and snorted a frustrated breath. "How could I get away with that? The first thing men ask on a date is 'what do you do'?"

"Tell him you're a doctor. It's the truth."

"He already knows that. The next thing he's bound to ask is my specialty."

"Make something up."

"Right." She sipped her tea. "He's not dumb."

"No, but he's distractible."

Ava nodded slowly and mulled Lorna's argument. All these years she'd believed in being upfront about her profession. Believed in laying it all out on the table and letting the chips fall where they may.

Where had it gotten her?

An expense-paid trip to Nowhere and a mouthful of dirt when the men made tracks.

She never thought she'd resort to subterfuge to kindle a relationship but she'd been kicked in the shins too many times when men found out what she did. Most of them reacted as if she was a prostitute, for crying out loud.

But she wasn't. She was, as Gage would say, a Prostate-tute.

Irony thinned her lips. She'd specialized in proctology to fulfill a promise to her dying father. Whodathunk that decision would brand her not only unfuckable, but unlovable to every other man on the planet.

"Okay." Her shoulders slumped as she glanced at Lorna. "I won't tell him."

* * * * *

The minute Arnie entered Harry's Hangaround later that evening he knew he'd been set up. There she sat at the Archer table, in lunar-white glory, looking literally out of this world.

Arnie's head started spinning. Whoa, Nellie! He seriously needed to get a grip. What were the odds of an alien invasion? Had to be astronomical. Right now, he needed to focus. He was being set up for breeding, er, romance. Best to squirm out of that frying pan first.

Although unsure about the outcome, he recalled the field test he often used to eliminate improbable mates, saving time and money. It usually took less than thirty seconds to unmask them as intellectual lightweights. Even Gage respected The Test.

Mentally tucking it away for later, he traversed the restaurant, trying not to make eye contact with *It*. Every time he met that unearthly gaze, he grew bewitched. Tonight he wanted a clear head.

Lorna stood up and kissed him. "You've already met Dr. Ava Ward," she said. "My friend from Minneapolis."

Yeah. Yeah. He didn't need Lorna to remind him she was a doctor. He knew that already and that simply meant she worked hard and had good study habits—if she was dim enough to need them. Having a medical degree did not make her smart. "How you doing?" he asked. "Did you get settled?"

"I did. Gage and Lorna have a lovely home."

It was a bald lie and everyone knew it, but Arnie let her get away with it since she was most likely trying to fit in with the humans.

"Join us," she invited.

Arnie had no choice but to sit next to her. It'd been carefully engineered that way. But he made sure his leg didn't brush hers for more than an instant and he made his best effort to stay clear of her misty perfume.

In a throwback to the encounter at the airport, he couldn't think of a word to say.

He sensed Ava turn in his direction. "So you're Gage's mechanic," she mentioned in a leading way.

Arnie nodded, reaching for the bread. "That's right."

"Lorna said you majored in aeronautics at MIT."

"Among other things. And you studied at Columbia," he said to trip her up. He knew very well it'd been Harvard.

Ava nodded.

Ah ha!

"That's where I got my MS in Astrophysics."

Arnie's spine fused. She studied the physical and chemical constitution of celestial matter. Was that considered "med school" where she came from?

"It's just a hobby." She shrugged and took a sip of beer. "I had some time to kill."

*Kill what?*

"Ava never had to waste a minute hitting the books like the rest of us dweebs," Lorna laughed, gazing fondly at The Entity.

Could the situation get any worse?

The hour for The Test drew nigh. "Oh yeah?" he asked in a tone of friendly challenge. "Let me ask your learned opinion on something then."

Across the table, Gage perked up. He'd heard that lead-in many times before and was obviously interested in what Ava's answer would be.

"Shoot," Ava said, catching the challenge with a strange glitter in her eyes.

Arnie half turned to face her. He felt a slow smirk begin around his lips. "Can you prove time exists?"

The glitter in her eyes went out and she got a bored expression on her face. "No."

Her answer wasn't what he expected. Gage raised his eyebrows. Arnie ignored him. "Why?"

Ava shrugged. "Because it doesn't. Everyone knows that. It's just a device to measure light," she continued, unasked. "We've assigned numbers that mean nothing to a lifecycle we scarcely understand."

The situation just got worse.

She giggled. "Time was invented by someone with too much light on his hands."

Arnie laughed his head off.

Much worse.

So far, he'd managed to skirt the love thing quite nicely. He didn't really believe in all that sap anyhow because he'd reached thirty-four years of age with his heart fully intact. The odds of that happening to the average American Male had to be through the roof. Therefore, love couldn't exist.

Simple logic.

But then, he'd never met anyone who possessed a heavenly body *and* a mind that moved at warp speed.

He could handle a close encounter with the pretty white-haired body snatcher, as long as she didn't try to eat him afterward. But could he see her back to the mother ship after the wedding knowing their combined IQs equaled the angle of a circle?

"What's your specialty?" he asked, more as a distraction from his misgivings than out of any particular interest. Ripping a bite of bread from the loaf and reaching for the butter, he tried to calm his frazzled nerves. *Probably In-Vitro Fertilization.*

Lorna and Ava exchanged glances. Arnie fired a look at Gage. His shoulders shook in silent laughter. Something sinister slithered up Arnie's back. What were they up to?

Before Ava could answer, Lorna cleared her throat. "I'm starved," she declared too perkily. "I think I'll order the BBQ. What're you getting, Ava?"

The waitress arrived and took their orders. The women immediately retired to the powder room, leaving Arnie in suspended animation with a Cheshire-faced Gage.

\* \* \* \* \*

Ava bolted the door to the tiny, dingy bathroom and turned to Lorna. "I can't do it."

"Yes, you can."

"I can't lie to him. He's too sweet."

Lorna folded her arms across her chest in the take-charge way commonly used by Judith, her overbearing mother. "You're not lying. You're withholding information."

"It's the same thing and you know it."

"I do not," Lorna said stubbornly. She pulled the ponytail elastic out of her long, sable hair and neatened it with a comb. "It makes you mysterious. Arnie'll eat that up. He loves puzzles."

Ava sighed at herself in the mirror. "I'm an open book."

"And that's part of your problem. You slam men with information about yourself. It's scary."

"So now the truth is scary?"

Lorna snorted. "The truth about you is. Besides the proctology factor, you're too smart for your own good."

"Arnie can handle smart."

"But I doubt he can handle a proctologist." Lorna shrugged. "Care to find out? Be my guest."

Ava rested her hands on the countertop. No way. Not yet. Never mind the soul mate part, she wanted to at least get laid this week.

"Thought so. Just distract him whenever he broaches the topic."

She came to life again. "It won't work. He's bound to find out even if this doesn't go anywhere, which I seriously doubt it will."

"What?" Lorna stared her down in the mirror. "You're putting the kibosh on this thing before it's even gotten off the ground? Please!"

"Face it, Lorna. I live in Minneapolis!"

"That's what airplanes are for—if we can coax Arnie into one once in while."

"What's that supposed to mean?"

Lorna mumbled something under her breath. Ava gave her shoulder a push. "Spill."

"He's still scared of flying. Gage recently made him get his license but he won't use it."

Ava threw up her hands. "Oh wonderful. An airplane mechanic who's scared to fly." She pinched the bridge of her nose. "These things could only happen to me. What's the use?"

"Do you want a soul mate or not?"

Ava nodded. Heart-achingly so. More than anything, really. She'd been so lonely.

"You'll never find him with that attitude. Arnie is it for you. I know it."

"Well, he won't be when he finds out I lied to him," argued Ava. "I know I'd hate it if he lied to me."

Lorna finished her ponytail and spun to clasp her friend's shoulders in both hands. She gave her a little shake. "He won't stick around long enough to hate you if you tell him what you do for a living. Arnie's slightly, er, phobic."

"About what besides flying?" Ava shrilled.

"Everything."

"Now you tell me."

"He's getting better."

"For heaven's sake, Lorna. Proctology is a perfectly decent livelihood. I love my job! Why should I fib about it?"

"Because it'll scare the pants off him the same way it has all your potential lovers."

The two women locked eyes, hands flying up to their mouths as a gaggle of giggles erupted.

"Don't," Ava gasped. "Don't start with Gage's corny puns."

They laughed harder.

"I'm just being proctical, Ava…" Lorna's voice trailed off into hysterical laughter.

"Stop," Ava cried, hands gripping her aching sides. "I need a tissue." She felt around the counter, trying through a glaze of tears to find the complimentary tissue box Harry thoughtfully provided.

"You've turned his head…" Lorna coughed.

That did it. Ava flew into a stall and sat down on the cool porcelain bowl. When she saw Lorna approach the stall door, she slammed it shut and locked it, jamming her fingers in her ears. "I can't hear you, I can't hear you," she singsonged.

\* \* \* \* \*

Back at the table Gage appeared strangely subdued. Arnie's eagle eye spotted several lip twitches followed by a careful schooling of features. He knew better than to try to get Gage to fess up. The man could keep secrets safer than a bank vault when he wanted to.

The women returned to the booth suspiciously red-eyed and flushed. Arnie rose to let Ava slide in. The brush of her bare arm against his sent a chatter of Morse code into his crotch. It didn't take a rocket scientist to decipher the desperate SOS. Arnie forgot his original question.

"What do you think of Harry's?" Gage asked conversationally.

Her green gaze opened wide and spread its eerie light around the restaurant. "Can't beat the propeller ceiling fans," she said. "Are all those parts on the wall leftovers from crash scenes?"

Arnie almost snorted beer through his nose. "Yeah," he said, recovering. "Over there is what's left of the *Jenny Jones*—a bum tail rotor." He leaned closer, allowing her fresh, meadowy scent to envelope him. "To your left are the remains of Ron Gibson's poor Cessna. It took elbow grease, but we got most of Ron off."

Ava laughed out loud—a surprising sound coming from such a wraith. And she looked really pretty when she did, not in the least bit nitrogen-deprived with those flushed cheeks and lively eyes.

Arnie couldn't recall ever making a female laugh and was completely bowled over by how good it felt. His cock noticed too.

Shifting uncomfortably in his seat to give Saturn Five more room on the launch pad, his lower leg found hers under the table and flat out refused to exit the area.

The Space Invader responded by sliding her long appendage gently over his and wrapping it around slowly, like a tentacle.

Saturn Five's liquid hydrogen achieved flight pressure. Arnie let loose a lazy grin.

T-minus ten and counting.

# CHAPTER TWO

No way he'd played footsie with ET, Arnie reflected the second he woke up the next morning.

Did he?

Reaching overhead, he flipped open a blind, peering out the window at the pinking sky and trying to fathom what had happened last night.

Sure, he believed in other intelligent life forms. But the chances of a hot and willing space babe slithering right into his pocket protector had to be way out there with the odds against Apollo Thirteen returning safely to Earth.

And yet, that had happened.

Throwing back the sheet in frustration, he got up and prowled into the bathroom. The grimacing contortions of his face in the mirror held a moment's fascination while he brushed his teeth—outward manifestations of what *she* did to his sex drive.

A frustrated growl quaked his chest as he turned on the shower. In his most spine-tingling fantasies, he never imagined encountering something like Ava. Whatever that something might be.

While the room steamed up from the shower and thoughts of her, the pressure in his cock built to the unbearable level of last night. Stepping under the spray, he reached for the soap and slicked up his hands, grabbing his hard shaft and stroking with well-practiced velocity.

Closing his eyes, he imagined the hot water trickling down his flesh was her white hair. He recalled how soft it'd felt between his fingers. Would the hair around her pussy be as soft?

As billowy and blissful against his cheeks as he licked her clit into a hard, throbbing nub, against his aching cock as it inched slickly inside her?

Would the hot, wet skin inside her pussy be as succulent and tight as the skin on the rest of her, the muscles as pert and firm around his pumping shaft? The voices inside his head told him *yes*. She would be as unusual in bed as she was out.

Prickles of approaching orgasm charged through his balls. His free hand cupped his firm head while the long, insistent strokes of the other hand on his shaft increased to a blistering pace. Ringing his head with his fingers, the molten juices inside bubbled and oozed.

Within moments Saturn Five launched majestically. Arnie's hips bucked and he heard her name burst out of his throat and into the steamy, airless room. It seemed to mingle with the sticky wet dew on the tiles then drip down from the ceiling until it coated him like paint.

Hot cum arced into his hands, spurt after spurt shooting wicked jolts of pleasure down his legs and through his mind. Then it mingled with the soap and water and swirled down the drain.

He took a recovering breath and rested his forehead against cool tiles while mindlessly sudsing the rest of his body. Some dusty corner of his brain registered that she couldn't have possibly blown in from the outer limits, but the feelings and sensations she aroused in his soul were as alien as if she had.

Still, Earthling or not, the MD after her name stood for *major deviant* and her miraculous appearance merited further investigation.

Emerging from the shower to get dressed, he frowned when the phone rang. Probably one of the siblings calling to complain about a spent light bulb or a broken computer or one of the many other dopey problems they liked pestering him with.

He snatched the receiver while tugging up his jeans. "What!"

"Lorna wants you over for dinner tonight," Gage said. "Six o'clock."

Arnie pulled a T-shirt over his head. "Why?" Like he didn't already know.

"Ava wants to stargaze."

*Stargaze, my ass. She's homesick.* "Okay," he snorted. "I'll bring the 'scope."

"Later." Gage hung up.

Slapped back to reality, Arnie sat down on the edge of his bed to tie his work boots. Tonight would end in yet another crudely concealed attempt to breed him with Thing. Though he wanted to, badly, he disliked being forced into mating rituals by others. He always felt scrutinized, as if he was on stage performing. It was a strange feeling that had followed him around his whole life, making him freeze up and look around at odd moments, the hair on his arms at attention. And that was the main reason he'd beaten a hasty retreat last night.

Even though the footsie segment had been the most fun he'd had in months, he'd felt someone watching. Again. And not just Lorna and Gage. A quick glance around the Hangaround had proved him wrong for the umpteenth time. But he couldn't shake the creepy feeling. Never could.

As a result of its omnipresence in his life, he normally didn't go in for casual sex, and certainly wasn't into PDAs. So *could* he fuck her, no matter how willing she seemed?

*Chrysler.*

How the Sam Hill could he fuck her when he couldn't even make eye contact without freaking? She was so awesomely variant, so close to flawless in both mind and body, he mortally feared Saturn Five's boosters would fail, dashing everyone's hopes for a successful blastoff.

If that happened, being needled at the Hangaround would be bad enough. What if The Entity blabbed back home and his poor performance became some sort of giant, cosmic joke?

He shuddered.

Gage had shenanigans on the brain too. And last night he'd definitely withheld important information. If only Arnie could figure out what.

He'd known Gage for a lifetime. Since Lorna came along he'd been aware of a widening breach in their friendship. He'd put it down to the fact that Gage was busy forging a bond with the future missus. As sad as it seemed, these things happened. But now his thoughts transected different circles.

As soon as *she* arrived, Lorna and Gage started acting strangely, almost like different people. He flinched.

Maybe they were *all* homesick.

Could Gage and Lorna have been swapped out? They hadn't been around much lately. Her computer had been acting up. Was that because of her new magnetic field? And didn't he see an unusually bright light in the sky a few nights ago?

Nah, he shook his head. Couldn't be. Better flambé the flights of fancy before they carted him away. On a whim, he picked up the phone again, punching in his sister's number. "You busy?" he asked when he heard Nora say hello.

* * * * *

Ava awakened with a pant to a slick, sticky puddle between her legs. No way had she gotten her period. She probed her sopping crotch with two fingers and raised them to look at the white cream coating the tips.

A wet dream? Her whole body zinged with the charge of fresh sex. She felt invigorated. Alive. And it wasn't because of the clean country air seeping in through the open window. Idly, she sucked her fingers, enjoying the flavors and scents of the body she knew so well.

Too well.

It was all she'd had lately. And it would quite possibly have to make do for the time being. If Arnie's track speed was any indication.

She couldn't figure out where she'd gone wrong last night. He'd certainly been willing to engage in prolonged touchy-feely under the table. His strong hand had rested on her thigh, tentatively at first, but then with increasing, erotic pressure. Their hips had collided and squirmed, the hard, tense feel of his muscles working her steadily into a lather of sweaty need.

Then he'd bolted into the night, leaving her, Lorna and Gage gagging on his dust.

But she was still hot for him.

How could she not be after the mental and physical connections they'd made so easily? First at the airport, then with his quirky test—which she'd been thrillingly aware was a test. Geeks did that all the time. Geeks like *her*.

She stroked her wet fingers along her labia, parting the folds and finding the sensitized nub of her clit. Her pussy still throbbed and her legs trembled. She'd definitely come in her sleep.

Closing her eyes she heard the faint muffled sounds of Lorna and Gage having morning sex. The soft steady beat of a headboard against the wall, small gasps, stifled groans. And her body quickened again to the noises. Suddenly she wanted to join them. She wondered what would happen if she appeared naked in their room. Would they startle and stop, reaching frantically for the covers?

Or would they motion her over?

Ava considered herself purely monogamous, but as the trickle of liquid heat in her pussy dribbled out over her probing fingers, she let the harmless fantasy take flight. Scrabbling in her suitcase for her vibrator, she inserted Arnie into the scene. In her mind there were two beds side by side. She and Arnie entwined on one watching Lorna and Gage fuck madly on the other.

Good God.

Lubricating the end of the jelly cock in her own juices, she slid it inside her gasping pussy and flicked on the switch.

*Lorna's legs on Gage's shoulders and him high on his arms pumping hard into her cunt.*

The vibrator inside Ava morphed into Arnie's swollen cock. She twirled it, dipped it, in and out, slowly at first while imagining the sounds. The growls and whimpers of two people fucking. Four people fucking. Watching each other. Being watched. Fucking.

Her hips rose high into the air and her legs fell open in a split. Arnie's cock rammed into her, plunging, circling. She grabbed her down pillow and hugged it tightly to her body. For this moment, it became his body. His warm flesh against hers while they humped.

His balls slapped her ass, his eyes dark and swirling. She felt his tongue fuck her mouth and she sucked on it.

*Gage on his back and Lorna on top, his hands lifting her and his cock thrusting up to spear her.*

Every nerve in her body began humming and bouncing. Her pussy clenched Arnie's rod until it couldn't get out. But still it thrummed relentlessly inside her. Grazing her G-spot and whispering against her clit.

Before reason escaped her completely, she thrust the down pillow into her mouth and came with great heaving moans even as she heard Lorna and Gage orgasming simultaneously in the next room. Her legs dangled helplessly in the air, her torso thrashed and she imagined Arnie bucking in ecstasy, his steaming cum coating her pussy and singeing her keening nerves.

With a gasp she fell back against damp sheets. For a moment she allowed herself to believe Arnie's breath blowing over her superheated flesh. In reality it was the cool morning breeze from the open window. The fantasy sunk into a hollow place in her stomach.

God. She wished she could have more sex. But not only that. She wished she could have it with someone who understood what she said when she opened her mouth. Someone who'd been just as lonely in this world as she.

Someone like her.

\* \* \* \* \*

"I can't believe he hit the road like that," Lorna fumed over brunch. She wore a silky red robe that contrasted beautifully with her mink-brown hair. Gage sat beside her looking rumpled and content.

Overexposed in the bright sunlight streaming into the kitchen, Ava had a sudden urge to wash this morning's extreme-for-her fantasy away in the shower. She'd heard people having sex before. Happened all the time in the dorms at Harvard and rarely if ever affected her libido. What had gotten into her today? "We have to stop him next time," she sighed, taking a bite of toast and reminding herself that at least Arnie found her pale hair intriguing.

All through college she'd wished for another color, changing it every month with the help of drugstore dyes. Finally, she'd accepted it. She discovered men generally found white hair alluring, what inevitably sent them running was her profession.

Wasn't it ironic that men could be gynecologists and no one batted an eyelash? Let a woman go into proctology and the world figured she was deviant.

Ava hoped desperately that Arnie would be different. Certainly, he had the intelligence to understand, but hey, she was realistic. Assholes were highly emotional areas to men. And they thought women were freaky about vaginas.

"Can you believe he didn't ask her out?" Lorna asked Gage, still gnawing her bone.

He grinned at Ava. "He will."

Lorna looked from Gage's smug smile to Ava's arched brow and back again. Her eyes narrowed. "What's going on?"

Gage grinned. "When I went out for donuts this morning, I caught him at the Emporium. He was buying a shitload of clothes with two of his sisters."

They had to peel Lorna up from the floor. "Buying clothes? Shopping with his *sisters*?" She pinned a meaningful look on Ava. "This is serious. He never wears anything but T-shirts and jeans. He wants to look good for you."

"He will in the orange shirt," Gage mumbled through a mouthful of toast. "Went with his hair."

Lorna brushed crumbs off his chest. "Since when have you become a metrosexual?"

"Hey, give me some credit," Gage said. "Arnie cleans up well. I noticed. The end."

The women smiled at each other. Ava could only imagine how cute Arnie looked, asking about colors and styles—those whimsical eyes so sincere. Her heart flopped over for a belly scratch.

"He asked about your plans today," Gage mentioned, sipping coffee.

"And you said?" Lorna asked.

"I ignored him."

"What?" She slapped his arm.

"Hey." He shrugged. "Arnie gets bored faster'n a tree at a termite reunion. Let him sniff her out."

Lorna got up and planted a big wet one on his mouth. Ruffling his hair, she turned to Ava. "See why I love him?"

Ava could only nod.

"He'll be over this evening, anyway, with the telescope. Should be a clear night."

Taking one last sip from the cooled dregs of her coffee, Ava rose. "Thanks for arranging that. I'll go get ready. Didn't you say something about giving me the grand tour of Flintlock?" she asked Lorna.

"Should kill five minutes," Lorna said.

Ava wandered back to Lorna's bathroom wondering if the sky would captivate her at all with Arnie hovering nearby. She'd had a lifelong passion for astrobiology and an evening studying the stars held the same fascination for her most people got from reading books. When she gazed into the night sky, worlds got built in her head, people were born, cultures formed and anything seemed possible.

At those moments her chest tightened with such yearning she could scarcely breathe. The pleasure-pain of wanting something, but not knowing what. Of sensing something out there, but not knowing where it was.

If she closed her eyes and wished with all her might, would it come to her? Would the heavens open and miraculous and unimagined things spill on the ground at her feet? And seeing them, would she know then what it was that caused such keening need?

Energy swirled into her midsection until she felt like she was going to explode. Adrenaline, her doctor side told her. Human beings were nothing but a container of chemicals. But a glance in the mirror at the vulnerability in her eyes said the energy must be something more. If only she knew what.

"It's a pretty day, we'll walk." Lorna popped into the bathroom while Ava applied the finishing touches to her makeup. When she popped back out to say goodbye to Gage, Ava borrowed the full-length mirror and checked herself out.

The new, snug bell-bottoms she'd bought had that trendy destroyed look. In a fit of giddiness, she'd purchased a silvery snakeskin tank top to wear with them, making her look like a sea urchin on acid. Ditching the Ray Bans, she slipped tiny blue rectangular glasses over her nose, slicked on a clear coat of lip gloss and figured if she survived Main Street USA for more than ten minutes, she was good to go for the duration.

"You look like a rock star!" Lorna paused at the doorway, mouth agape. "Stunning."

Ava turned with a smile. "Get out. I do not."

Lorna shook her head slowly. "Arnie's going to freak out."

"You just say that 'cause you love me." Ava squeezed Lorna's hard.

"Yeah, yeah." Lorna squeezed hard back. "I missed you, girl."

"Me too."

"Mascara check!" Lorna announced. A telltale puddle had appeared on her lids that Ava automatically reacted to. Four blotted eyes later they were out the door, braving the bright sunshine, gunning for action.

Two blocks later, they found *plenty*.

"Blink and you'll miss it," Lorna joked. "But there are a few neat antique shops. I found some good stuff."

Gage's home would need it too. He wasn't exactly a terrible decorator, he'd just lived alone too long.

Ambling along, they passed an ice cream parlor, a bookstore and the post office. Ava got itchy, but didn't break out in hives. That was good.

"There's Ye Olde Chocolate Shoppe," Lorna pointed out.

It was the location where Gage had proposed and altered the course of Lorna's life. She'd originally come to Flintlock to arrange a business merger with image consultant John Preston but had wound up merging with Gage instead.

Ava salaamed at the altar of chocolate making Lorna punch her arm in glee. She was bent over, waving her bottom around the sidewalk, when she heard Lorna giggle above her head.

"Hi Arnie! Ava dropped a contact. Quick, get down and help and for God's sake, don't move."

*I'm going to gut her. Gut her and hang her on the front lawn to dry.* "Whoa!" Her ass overbalanced and she started to list. A pair of firm, strong, all-too-masculine hands braced her hips. The urge to bump and grind in them nearly undid her. She imagined him pulling her back over his stiff, thick cock and humping her from behind. Right here on the street. In plain view. Like zoo animals.

What was it with these exhibitionist fantasies lately?

His hands cupped her cheeks and his thumbs wandered south like heat-seeking micro-missiles. Momma! The jolt of electricity powering through knocked her flat on her ass.

Arnie hunkered down next to her. "You all right?" His gaze flickered over her body.

"No, I mean yes. Oh forget it."

"Your sunglasses fell off." He handed them back, thought better of it and parked them on his own nose, peering at her over the top of the ridiculously small lenses. "I suggest that contact is history, daddy-o."

Ava stifled a moan of passion. He really did fit in with the beatniks. "That's okay," she muttered. "It was disposable."

Pushing hair out of her eyes, she looked at him. He watched her mildly for a second before reaching out and tugging them both to their feet.

If she possessed the wiles she wanted so badly, she'd have stumbled against him, just to see how he felt, but she waited too long, kicking herself when the moment passed.

"So, Arnie," Lorna said. "Gage said he saw you this morning. How's the family?"

"Myra's pregnant again. Nora's still trying." He cast a diffident glance in Ava's direction.

She rewarded him with a quick smile, raising her eyebrows to show interest. "Your sisters?"

"Yeah," he smiled crookedly back. "But you don't want to hear about those coconuts."

"I'd love to hear about your family," Ava said softly.

Lock and load. His gaze drew a bead on hers. The impact knocked her into startled retreat. He advanced, his expression intensifying and…glowing.

She swallowed hard.

A bright silver light shot out of his eyes and washed her in a peculiar bath. She stared, caught like a deer, mouth opening and closing as magnetic energy lasered into her pupils, looped through her body, lassoed her brain and wrenched her into his force field.

"I was heading to the diner for lunch. You wanna tag along?"

Did he say something? It sounded like underwater gobbledygook.

"Thanks but no thanks. We just ate," Lorna snipped.

"Ice cream," he countered.

"Gotto go. See you, Arnie. Bye!" Lorna yanked Ava down the street. She tripped over her own feet, head spinning like a crazed carousel.

"Maybe later," she managed over her shoulder. Arnie's demeanor turned predatory as they cantered away. Stiff and alert.

*Focused.*

Ava got the heebie-jeebies. The good kind. And suddenly wished for another private moment with her jelly cock. "Slow down, hey! Why'd you do that?" She pulled Lorna under an awning and leaned against the brick storefront for support. "I wanted to have lunch with him." *And fuck him black-and-blue on the dessert cart.*

"Of course you did," Lorna said. "But more importantly, so did he." She snuck a glance out onto the sidewalk. "Coast is clear. Phew, that was close." She gazed at Ava triumphantly. "He's salivating. Couldn't have asked for better timing. His radar caught that locomotion all the way across the street and he risked life and limb to get to it."

"No way."

"Way." Lorna said. "I saw the whole thing. He broke land-speed records. You're in his sights now."

"Speaking of sight, his eyes were, um…" It sounded nutty, even to her. Maybe she'd imagined the whole thing as a byproduct of intense attraction.

"Oh yeah. His 'mood eyes'."

"Mood eyes? Like, mood rings?" Her jaw slackened.

Lorna nodded. "When he's really happy, they turn silver. When he's unhappy, they're almost black. Most of the time they're that weird bronze color. You made him happy."

"*Mood* eyes?" She shut her lids and tried shaking it into her mind. *Impossible.*

"That's what he calls them," Lorna said absently. "Arnie's not like us."

Did her blood just turn to slush? *Me either.* When she opened her eyes Lorna stood enshrouded in a white halo. Ava blinked and the halo went away. "He took my sunglasses. I can't stand this glare. Let's go find him." *And find out* what *he is.*

"Nice try. Just swivel that pretty face around and take a look at where you are."

Ava stepped back a few paces, peered up at the old brick façade and let herself be distracted for a moment — this was, after all, Lorna's party. "Well, I'll be darned," she muttered. Preston's Emporium, the home of Lorna's ex-business partner. "Dare we go in?"

"We dare," Lorna said. "Everything's okay now. You can get sunglasses, socks, laxatives. Anything your heart desires."

"Lead the way."

They met the extensive Preston clan of half-cousins thrice removed, and enjoyed the down-home flavor of penny candy. They oohed and ahhed over the selection of flip-flops, had a soda at the old-fashioned counter, and skimmed the latest issue of *Superman*.

Ava thought she was going to throw up.

This was the sort of town she'd left behind in the far north, the sort of town she never wanted to see again. Unfortunately, it contained a man who jerked her in like a supermagnet.

Unable to keep her restless mind on any topic that didn't have the word *Arnie* in it, she asked, "Is the rest of his family as smart as he is?"

Lorna sent her a look that spoke volumes. "He's a total freakazoid to them. The black sheep."

"Whoa," Ava muttered, floored by the information. "Do they get along?" She and her parents had butted heads many times throughout her life. There were facets of her they just didn't get. They'd tried, though.

"He tries talking to them about the things they're interested in. His mechanical talents help. He fixes all their equipment." Lorna paused to try on a hairclip. "They give him a hard time about his brains, but they love him. It's just that after a while, he gets impatient. No one can come close to understanding him."

Ava's heart cracked. She knew what it felt like to be different from everyone else, to have people stop and stare. As much pleasure as her unusual looks and intelligence brought to her life that was how much they took away too. It was a bittersweet blessing. "He must be so lonely."

Lorna smiled sadly. "Sometimes I catch him when he's not looking—which is very hard to do, by the way. I swear he can read minds. But occasionally I see this sort of wistful expression on his face when he's with me and Gage. Of course, I could be totally misinterpreting it. Maybe it's more of a confused expression."

"Why did he stick around here?"

"Gage said he didn't want to work with a bunch of geeks in the armpit of the free world."

Ava laughed but her chest felt like a giant sunless cavern, and in the darkest, forlorn corner grubbed her heart. "He's a geek. But not."

Lorna nodded. "It's like he tries to deny his oddities. He tries to fit in. Like you."

God, she had this thirst to let him know she empathized and that he didn't have to worry about fitting in with others. He fit in with her.

But who was she kidding? He was perfectly happy before he met her and he'd be perfectly happy after she left. They both loved their work. They had lives. If they could manage a little togetherness for a while that'd be great. But what if they couldn't?

What if he didn't want to?

Well, that blew the lid off her pot. Maybe he would refuse a fling. Maybe footsie was as good as it got. Come to think of it, he avoided eye contact with her as much as possible. So much so that it had taken her aback when he finally looked at her.

"Tour's over," Lorna said, glancing at her watch. "We have just enough time to snag a cup of coffee before the fitting."

"I can't wait to see your dress," she murmured.

Although Lorna's side of the wedding would be small, she'd warned Ava the entire town would turn out for Gage. The reception would be held on Arnie's family farm—they'd slaughtered several hogs to roast in a pit.

Ava's throat started closing at the idea of a town-wide hoedown and the inane chatter required at receptions. But she'd get through it. She owed it to her best friend. Besides, she'd get a chance to meet Arnie's family, spend time with him, ask him why on God's green Earth he tinkered on toy planes for a living.

Meeting him had honed her hunger for mind-contact and it was driving her physical lust for him into deeper chambers than she'd initially planned on going. She had to keep reminding herself he was not her soul mate. He was a distraction. A sex toy. Because he had no ambition. The fact that he still lived in this town and not Houston was proof enough.

But even if he didn't want to work with other geeks in hot, steamy cities, there had to be a million companies that'd kill for an employee of his caliber. Something was wrong with this picture and Ava intended finding out what.

Plus, now that she'd experienced the potency of his gaze, she wanted it on her. All over her—while naked and chained…to a trapeze. And she planned on getting it. Tonight.

# CHAPTER THREE

Arnie sat on his couch watching Myra's kids run amok and fiddling with Ava's tiny blue sunglasses. For the umpteenth time, he checked his chronograph. T-minus sixty minutes. If he lived in New York it'd be time to go to Gage's. Then again, according to Galaxy Girl, time didn't exist.

A grin split his face. No one had ever passed The Test before, human or humanoid. The simple elegance of her deduction—contrasted with the stumbling, pompous discourses on gravity and bending light he usually got—stole his breath. Leave it to Ava to get it right. In his fantasies she sat next to him, cheerfully unraveling the Theory of Relativity. If anyone could do it, she could.

"Want me to hang these up for you?" Myra asked. He looked at her. She was holding his bag of new clothes.

"Nah. You need to get back."

"Not really," Myra said with a sigh. "Donny's gonna be late tonight. Want me to cook dinner for you?"

"I'm eating at Gage's."

Myra nodded. "I saw you talking to Lorna and a white-haired woman today. Someone new in town?"

Arnie warmed to the interest in his sister's tone. She rarely got off the farm. Just the fact that she'd stopped by this afternoon told him she felt lonely. "Yeah. Ava Ward. Her maid of honor."

"Never seen hair like that before."

*And you're not likely to, either.* "Nope."

"She gonna be at dinner too?"

Although not the sharpest crayon in the box, Arnie could plainly see curls of wax falling at his sister's feet. "She's into astronomy." He shrugged. "Gage asked me to bring the telescope over."

Myra hiked up an eyebrow. "I can see why you'd need new clothes, then."

Arnie met her eyes and they both smirked.

"She must really be something else."

*She's something else all right.* What a…what a…he searched for the right descriptive but the only one that popped into his head was "woman". Go figure. As if Ava was a mere mortal. He chuckled. But his cock got serious. *Woman.*

Ever since she'd done the hula in his hands, Saturn Five had been anxiously awaiting the go for main engine start. If that soft, round ass was an example of the rest of her anatomy, he might have to seal them both upstairs in his room for the weekend, where there was absolutely no chance of observation no matter what the hair on his arms said.

He launched off the couch with a restless groan and his three nieces glued themselves to his legs, waving fistfuls of clothing like banners. "Wear this one. No, this one!"

"I suggest you Tsetse flies calm down," Arnie said, peeling them off and crouching on his heels. They circled around him. "Let's see." He rummaged through the bag, pulling out the orange Hawaiian shirt. "What about this?"

The girls watched as he yanked off his T-shirt and shrugged into it. As a joke, he slipped on Ava's sunglasses. The nieces howled gales of approval.

"Where'd you get those?" Myra asked.

"Some spacey shop," he said, jogging into the bathroom to check out his look. The bright orange and turquoise shirt wasn't quite his style. But worn loose with the surf's-up puka shell necklace Nora'd grabbed, it looked passable.

He peered over the top of the sunglasses into the mirror. Not bad! Kind of cool, actually. He wondered if Ava would think so, figuring she probably would since they used to be hers.

While not exactly on top of fashion, he watched enough TV to know he looked good. Better make sure he smelled good too. People never knew when they stank to high heaven. It must be some ancient evolutionary device designed for population control.

All of a sudden, he didn't want to control those impulses in Ava tonight. Not that he wanted to add to the population, but he wouldn't say no to trying. Would he? He slapped on some aftershave, just in case.

"You smell fine," Myra said. He jerked back, startled that she'd followed him into the bathroom. "What's with you? I've never seen you so hepped up."

"No reason."

Myra shook her head and ruffled his hair. "How long has it been since Darla, six months?"

Sounded about right. Darla'd been whining about weddings, drooling for diapers. Arnie had nothing against those things, even wanted to get married someday. But not to Darla. Not to anyone he'd ever met.

"Ava Ward, huh?"

He nodded dopily.

"I dunno. The way you're acting, she might be the one."

He snorted. Wasn't it just the sweetest irony that the only person who ever gave him an atomic-sized inkling about marriage might not even be a person at all? How commitment phobic could you get?

Freud would have a frickin' field day with him.

"Well. I'll be skeddadlin' then."

For a second he thought he glimpsed a universe of knowledge in Myra's eyes.

"Tell the Tsetse flies I'll see them tomorrow." Something in his world had fragmented.

*T-minus fourteen minutes.*

**\* \* \* \* \***

"He's here, he's here." Lorna raced down the hallway and pounded on Ava's door. Even though Ava heard her coming at full gallop, she still startled at the sound.

"Let me in!"

"It's unlocked," Ava said drolly. Oh the dramatics!

"What are you wearing?" Lorna dived inside. "Oh my God." She skidded to a halt.

"Do I look all right?" Ava anxiously smoothed her skirt. For the big night, she'd selected an ice blue nylon tank top that fit like paint. As counterbalance, she wore a long white shimmery pencil skirt with an impressive fault line up the front. She'd shod her feet in slender, strappy flats in concession to Arnie's stature. She didn't want to look down at him — while vertical.

"You look like the arctic fox you are," Lorna murmured. "Stunning."

Ava heaved a sigh of relief. "Oh, thank you."

"Now hurry, he and Gage are in the backyard playing with their toys. I want you front and center when he comes in."

Ava followed her friend to the kitchen. Although the sun was setting behind the trees, casting long shadows across the grass, there was still enough daylight to catch a glimpse of him out in the yard. Her breath caught. "Get the bongo drums," she murmured.

"What?" Lorna looked up from the chicken breasts she was tenderizing.

"Never mind." Arnie looked like a dream. Ava's fingers came up to her neck to tease the braided silver chain she wore. Her heart throbbed a steady beat, quickening when she saw him toss back his head and laugh. He held a beer casually at his side, bringing it up to his lips for a sip and licking them afterwards.

*Baby, come to Momma.*

As Lorna warned earlier, the weight of her stare must have pressed down on him, for he shot a glance toward the sliding glass door.

When he saw her, he froze. The broad smile he wore faded and he simply stared, like yesterday at the airport. If she thought his eyes felt like a lick then, they were a definite slobber now.

Ava slanted her head and smiled, sending a small wave. In response, Arnie tilted his beer bottle in her direction and took a sip, his eyes never leaving her face. How unutterably suave. She determined then and there not to let those eyes stray away again. *You're mine, Rocket Man. Mine.*

"Well?"

Ava snapped around to see Lorna smiling kittenishly, pounding those breasts with extra zeal.

"Looks real tasty, doesn't he?" she asked.

"Oh Lorna. I've got to have him," Ava breathed.

"So you shall, my dear. So you shall. Gage is grilling him right now."

"Grilling him?"

Lorna tossed back her hair, which she uncharacteristically wore loose. "About his intentions."

"Puhlease!" Ava cried.

"Shhh. He'll hear you. Gage knows what to say. By tonight, if Arnie hasn't made a move, at least we'll have some insider information."

"There ought to be a law," Ava joked.

"A law against that outfit," Gage quipped, coming into the room. "What do you think, Arnie, is Ava's outfit legal?"

Arnie stepped over the threshold and freed one of his sly grins. "I suggest shrink-wrap should be outlawed as clothing.

Too hard to rip off." His gold-flecked eyes lapped her body before returning to her face. They grew silvery again as he sauntered over. "You look nice," he said.

"So do you," she whispered.

As if the idea of him ripping the shrink-wrap off wasn't hot enough to handle, the fabric of his shirt brushed against her nipple and she caught a whiff of freshly scrubbed engineer. She moved to get away, unwilling to faint on him, and this time guilelessly stumbled.

"Watch out." He looped an arm around her waist, bringing her tight against his chest. Her nose stopped centimeters from his, lips a head tilt away.

His grip tightened, fingers kneading her flesh before loosening and sliding up an inch. Ava laid a hand across his well-developed pecs and caught his heart beating frantically. Like hers.

*Gimme some tongue. Just do it.* And sure enough, his head swiveled slightly, dipping lower. His hand tightened until she could almost feel whether he was as horny as she…

"Crudités!" Lorna chirped, setting out a tray of munchies.

"You okay now?" he asked softly.

"Mmm-hmm," she murmured.

"Sure?" He breathed the word into her hair.

"Yeah," she sighed, tucking a strand behind her ear and peering through lowered lashes.

He smiled. "Not going to fall down?"

"Mmm-mmm."

"Then it's safe to let you go?"

Ava started to move away. He pulled her back. Their hips collided and Ava got her answer. He was as aroused as she.

"You didn't answer. Is it safe to let you go?"

Ava dipped her face, feeling a hot flush creeping up her neck. "It's safe," she purred, glancing up again. "But unwise."

He chuckled. "She has to go and challenge my common sense."

"Far be it from me," she giggled sotto voce.

Now his other arm came around, cradling her against his engorged cock with tacit demand. His forehead brushed hers. "Why'd you run away this afternoon?" he asked in a barely audible voice. "I wanted to eat with you."

She squirmed as liquid lust dribbled into her panties. "Lorna made me." It seemed natural to nuzzle his neck, drape an arm around his shoulder.

"I suggest you tell her to butt out," he said, lifting her chin with one hand while the other slid down to lace fingers.

Ava moaned as their fingers mated, showing what he would feel like and move like inside her. "I will."

"Promise?" The tips of their noses grazed, fresh breath fanning her face.

"I—

He kissed her the minute her mouth opened, capturing her lower lip and sucking it before covering her mouth with his. Tactile lips held an intimate candlelight dinner, sampling, sipping, feeding. His tongue slipped in for a tentative taste, flicking her teeth and upper lip then venturing in farther to skim along the roof of her mouth.

Good Lord. She never realized she had a G-spot in there. The hard tip of his tongue stroked back and forth along the center rim of her palate and an electrified hunger whirled through her. He carried in a pleasant aftertaste of expensive, micro-brewed beer which acted like an astringent in her mouth, clearing out all other flavors and leaving her ready for his.

She eagerly lapped it up.

He feasted on her like a gourmet, so tenderly her knees buckled in surrender. Sensing her weakness, his hand untwined and advanced to the small of her back, arching her into his swollen erection.

"Gage and Lorna…" she moaned.

"Gone," he answered. "Probably watching from the yard."

*Watching*. Her pulse beat the band. He deepened the kiss, tongue tangling with hers. A furious gust of heat opened her legs, parting the front slit in her skirt so only a thin barrier of nylon panty protected her mound. She tilted her hips and wiggled to hug his shaft in the warmth of her labia.

Every muscle in his body coiled. She could hear them screaming like a stadium full of fans. His hands charged into her skirt, fingers grazing her outer thighs, kneading her ass, scooping down and under as they had earlier on the street—as if he intended hoisting her up to ride his cock.

She wouldn't have said no.

*Watching*.

Through the slippery fabric of her panties, the heat from his demanding fingertips dripped the length of her crack, hesitating at the blazing, wet entrance to her cunt, and then torturing her by not touching but by sliding out of her skirt and up her back around to her breasts. She slumped into them urgently, needing his pinch on her nipples. But he gently pushed her up.

"Later," he whispered, face buried in her neck.

"Don't do this to me," she whimpered.

"To *you*?" he chuckled, lifting his head to gaze into her eyes. "I'm about to blow an O-ring. I suggest Lorna wouldn't appreciate the mess."

Reconnaissance time. They both turned slightly toward the sliding door, but all they could see were themselves in the glass.

*Watching*.

His gaze met hers in the reflection. Like a child discovering a mirror for the first time, he stroked his hand down her hair and watched as she arched her neck and purred into his touch. He looked at her, then back at her reflection until she too became mesmerized by the ghostly images in the glass.

"I'll have to add one large mirror to my shopping list," he said. "Would you like that?"

Her eyes rolled back in her head in bliss.

"I know I'd like to watch while we do it."

"Tonight?" she asked desperately.

His gaze bored into her, flashing with heat and unanswered questions. "Is that what you want?"

What was he asking? If she wanted a one-night stand? If she wanted him? Ava blinked, unsure how to answer, afraid that whatever she said might be misinterpreted.

She finally stammered noncommittally. "Not just tonight."

Some of the flash cooled out of his brimstone eyes and he swept a strand of hair off her cheek. "Good," he said. "It's going to take a lot more than one night to do everything I have planned for you."

A hot, erotic surge liquefied her core. She leaned against him, dropping her head onto his shoulder. Arnie rested a cheek on hers briefly before lifting her chin again and caressing her mouth in one last, sweeping kiss.

Then he patted her ass. "They're outside at the BBQ grill. I wonder what they're thinking."

Ava raised her face to meet his dark, knowing gaze.

"I could hazard a guess," she replied.

"Gage gave me the Spanish Inquisition earlier."

Ava twittered. "I know. Lorna and I were going to plan our strategy based on his notes."

"Like you needed one," he teased. "You knocked me on my ass the minute you hit the tarmac."

"You melted my panties too."

Arnie groaned, clapping his forehead in agony. "Don't say things like that. I might do something that'd get me arrested."

"Too late," Ava quipped. "The passion police are already on the way."

With a wicked, wide grin, he shook his head and shoved his hands into his pockets. "This is going to be quite a ride. Come on, let's join the sane."

"I better freshen up first."

"Don't be long," he said, sounding like he'd be waiting for her. In bed.

*Omigod omigod.* Ava rested shaking hands on the countertop in the bathroom. He was incredible, amazing, so much more than she'd expected. And this was just a public appetizer, a drop in the bucket of what he might do in private.

She stared at the mess in the mirror. Her cheeks were pink from his kisses, lips full and glistening. Her hair, well, did someone say *train wreck?*

Grabbing Lorna's comb, she untangled the knots, fluffing it and releasing Arnie's spicy scent. She had to sit down on the toilet. *Was it hot in here?* She flicked on the fan and leaned back against the cold porcelain tank. Gulping air and trying to bring her respiration back to semi-normal levels, she smoothed her skirt with her hands and rested them on her achy mound.

Of their own accord, long fingers started edging underneath the damp elastic of her panties. Her legs spread open and she pressed a fingertip against her hot, throbbing clit. A mental image of him standing just outside the bathroom door, intent, listening, head bowed with unfulfilled desire, spurred her finger into furious, determined circles. She yearned for the thrust and jiggle of her vibrator, tucked safely into her suitcase — so close and yet so far. But within seconds her well-trained fingers had massaged her clit to the peak, and she tumbled over, biting her lip to keep from crying his name.

She felt pretty sure she failed.

This orgasm wouldn't quit — kept heaving through her in wave after wave. She was so saturated with Arnie, so primed for his body, so aware of his sharply focused attraction she'd been in a continual state of arousal since she hit Flintlock.

How on earth would she make it through dinner without jumping his bones?

And to think she'd thought he was *sweet*. My Lord. The man was one hot tamale. That tongue, those hands, those lips.

Yet he presented with such innocence. Little Arnie Simpson, the country boy, the hog farmer's son. *Hogwash*! He knew his way around a woman like he knew his way around an airplane. Expertise seeped from his fingertips like motor oil.

Ava could not *wait* to fuck him.

\* \* \* \* \*

*Terminal Launch Sequence activated.*

Hearing the muffled torture of her orgasm through the door, Arnie drew a ragged breath, adjusted his pants and slapped on a fake smile before joining Gage and Lorna. He could get through the evening, he could. If the imprint of Ava hadn't branded his dick.

What had happened just now? What had driven him to listen at the bathroom door? He'd never done that before. Never had any interest in hearing a woman use the toilet. But he'd instinctively known that wasn't what she was going to do.

Almost as if she'd told him. As if a text message had scrolled across his brain.

*Masturbation alert! Masturbation alert!*

It'd taken all the strength he possessed not to barge through the door and take her pleasure into his own hands.

He'd intended playing it cool, maintaining a professional distance to get to know The Enemy. But once she'd splashed down in his arms, all bets were off. The little men in the command module had a separate agenda—they wanted out.

"Everything okay?" Lorna asked sweetly when he appeared on the lawn.

Arnie didn't bother to reply. Instead, he tossed her a warning look and scrounged in the ice chest for another beer. She snickered behind his back. Some friend.

"These breasts look mighty tender," Gage intoned. "And would you look at that, juicy too."

Lorna laughed outright. At least Gage had the decency to hide it.

"Cut it out," Arnie growled.

"My, my. In a bad mood, are we?" Lorna tsked. "And after those incredible fireworks. Such a shame."

"Arnie's disappointed he didn't see the grand finale," Gage mentioned. "You know, when they shoot off the really big ones."

"I suggest you can it. Ava will be embarrassed."

"Oh, *Ava* will be embarrassed. I see. Gage, honey. *Ava* will be embarrassed."

Arnie threw himself into a lawn chair and scowled at the emerging stars. His frown eased as he began wondering which one gave birth to Ava. Could he go back with her? he mused. Knowing with startling clarity that if it came down to it, he might.

"There's Venus," he said just as the door slid open and she appeared.

"You flatter me," Ava smiled, crossing the lawn with a seductive gait and pulling up a chair.

Arnie flopped his head back and reached out a hand. Her cool skin felt soothing—like nighttime and the sky. "After we eat, it's showtime."

"I can't wait." She shivered, rubbing her hands briskly up and down her arms. "I've missed the starry nights I remember from childhood."

In the deep recesses of Arnie's brain, a radar screen bleeped. "More stars where you came from?" he half-teased.

"Better visibility way up there. Of course, that was the only good feature. Might as well have been a vacuum, otherwise."

"You grew up in a vacuum?" A cold finger pressed his heart.

"Virtually," she laughed. "Outer space really, but don't tell anyone back home I said that."

*Of course not. They'd put you in the cryo tank for treachery.* His leg began to shake, fingers drumming nervously.

She turned to him, pale eyes and hair radiant, voice full of serenity. "Do you believe in other life forms?"

"You're asking me?" he croaked.

"Do you?" she repeated hypnotically. "I have to know, Arnie."

"Dinner!" Gage called.

Arnie sprang to his feet, folding up the lawn chair in a clatter of aluminum and shattering the web she'd been spinning.

"Oh! Are you all right?" Ava leapt up too, hovering in concern.

"Sure. Fine. Why?"

"You seem jumpy. Was it something I said?"

"You said something?" Best to plead ignorance. Maybe then his life would be spared when The Lizard King showed up to vaporize her for snitching.

"We were talking about where I grew up, other intelligent life."

"We were?"

"Arnie, how many beers did you have?"

*The perfect alibi.* "Five or six," he lied.

"Five or six? You better eat something. Come on." She helped right the chair and wrapped his arm around her before moving to the table. Her hair felt like moondust between his fingertips, milky skin glowing in the faded light.

Arnie swallowed hard in acknowledgment of this new information. She'd admitted her heritage. He was actually touching a being from another world. Not only that, she'd practically demanded to fuck him. Gage and Lorna were in on it too. They'd approved and encouraged the plan.

His head was about to explode.

Arnie'd never seen himself as a coward—except when it came to flying. But that had been an irrational fear that Lorna and Gage helped him overcome. *Lorna and Gage.* Lorna and Gage setting the stage, laying the groundwork to get him on the flying saucer.

Christmas on a cracker!

This went beyond a setup. It was a conspiracy!

Every ounce of common sense he had left screamed *beware*. He glanced at them. They were watching him, their eyes lit by embers on the grill.

They were *smiling*.

Taking a deep breath, Arnie considered his options.

A—stick around and see how it plays out.

B—consult the yellow pages for a twenty-four-hour psychoanalyst.

C—run like hell.

"Here's your plate," Lorna said, handing him dinner.

Argh! He'd lingered in indecisiveness too long. Oh well. What were his chances of outrunning The Outlander anyway? She could *coast* at light speed. He may as well eat first.

She sat down nearby and inched the chair closer, appendage brushing his. Saturn Five went on hold, recycling the countdown and confirming Arnie's worst fear—when push came to shove he wouldn't be able to engage in intergalactic congress, no matter how luscious and desirable the bait.

That put a damper on the evening.

Then again, here was the perfect time to institute Gage's motto, when life hands you a dilemma, make *dilemmanade*. The opportunity to stargaze with a creature that read the solar system like a roadmap didn't come down the pike too often.

His mood brightened a tad.

Inter-planet Janet was chirping happily with her minions. Once in a while, she squeezed his thigh. All was right with the world. For now. If nothing else, he'd get a first-rate education under her tutelage. If she devoured him in the morning, he'd emerge a smarter piece of shit.

He rubbed the corded muscles in his neck and drew a fatalistic breath. He was definitely in gimbal lock, unable to navigate through life anymore.

It was all part of the changeover process, he supposed, doubting he had a choice whether or not to follow her.

Gazing at luminous hair, twinkling eyes and sparkling skin, he resigned himself to fate. Sure as shooting stars, he was fucked.

# CHAPTER FOUR

"You have a Sky-Watcher?" Ava jiggled with excitement when he unveiled the telescope, running over to gape and slide a hand reverently along the glossy surface of the tube assembly. She turned bright eyes his way. "I've never stood this close to one."

'Cause you never had to, Arnie thought glumly, bending for a test peek. The scales of Libra popped into view, as if sending a cosmic laugh-gram over his imbalance since Jane Jetson zoomed in. He adjusted north and looped around the sky, searching for an interesting galaxy or nebula. When he came upon a kaleidoscopic swirl, he stepped back to let Ava strut her stuff. Astronomy wasn't his strongest point and he didn't feel like making more of a fool of himself than he already had.

Retiring to the ice chest for another brewski, he kept his distance while they peed all over themselves with wonder.

They acted like it was so new, so different, as if they'd never seen anything like it. Arnie took a good long gulp, trying to figure a way out of this mess. What was the use? He might as well enjoy these last hours on Earth, savoring the sound of her voice.

"What's wrong?"

He opened his eyes to see her looming with a Venusian halo ringing her head. "Nothing. Just thinking."

"About what?" She crouched at his feet, elbows perched on his knees, chin resting on folded hands. She looked too tasty for words and he couldn't resist reaching out to play with her hair.

"You."

She smiled impishly. "Can you be more specific?"

He lunged forward, capturing her chin and tilting her face right, then left into the moonlight. "Twinkle, twinkle little star," he whispered. "How I wonder what you are."

Ava giggled, not grasping his desperation. "Up above the world so high."

"Like a damn diamond in the sky." He cradled her face, brushing her hair away and gathering it into a ponytail at her neck. "Twinkle, twinkle little star, won't you tell me *what you are*?"

Mischief crept into her eyes and curled the corners of those succulent lips. "I can't."

"Why?"

"It'd frighten you away, like Miss Muffet."

"You're a fucking spider?"

Ava laughed.

"Really." Arnie ran his thumbs over her face, feeling the fine bones in her nose and cheeks, tracing her dark, arched eyebrows. "I know where you came from. Now tell me, what are you?"

"I'll only tell you if you promise not to run."

Oh boy. Denouement time. "Scout's honor." Since he'd never been a Boy Scout, it didn't count for much.

Ava sucked in a tense breath. Her guarded look ratcheted Arnie's nervousness by an order of magnitude. Then suddenly, she whooshed out incomprehensible words.

"I'm-Dr.-Ava-Ward-and-I'm-a-proctologist."

He sat back to decipher the message. She was Ava Ward, Probabilist. Okay. She believed that certainty in science was impossible. A lot of insiders did—him included. What was so scary about that? No grand confession there. "And," he queried, trying to draw her out. "That's important because?"

Ava fell silent. She looked confused, with her mouth opening and closing like that. "Well, it's what I do, who I am," she finally squawked. "It doesn't bother you?"

"Why should it?" If that's how she defined herself, who was he to question? Sure, he wanted more information. Eventually. "No biggie." He shrugged. "It's a reasonable science."

"You don't care?"

"Read my lips," he said, almost laughing at her relieved expression. "No."

She lit up like a flashlight, looking delirious and mesmerizingly sensual.

"Should I care?" he asked, falling under her spell yet again. Then he swatted air. "I suggest we drop it and move on." There were many, far more interesting topics he'd rather discuss.

But she didn't let go of it. "Lorna! I told him and he doesn't care!"

Lorna spun from the telescope. "You told him?"

The two women flew into each other's arms in a screaming frenzy. Twirling on the grass, they shrieked and hollered until Arnie thought for sure the men in black would be sniffing the air.

Had she really worried that much that a belief in probabilism would turn him away? Obviously so. Later, when he'd had time to adjust to her enthusiasm over the subject, he'd have to razz her. Right now, he was too horrified. In fact, he almost preferred the creeping terror of impending vivisection to this frantic, squealing joy.

"Can you believe this?" he asked Gage, pointing his beer at the display.

Gage plopped into a chair. "Not really," he said. "I thought for sure you'd wig out."

Arnie snapped around to gawk at him. He usually didn't throw his intellectual weight around, but Gage's words pissed him off. "I suggest you don't even know what it is."

Gage howled. "No man gets to be our age without knowing what *that* is," he snickered. "Unfortunately."

By then the girls had settled down and Lorna was eying him fondly. In a burst of affection, she threw herself on his lap and hugged his neck. "Oh Arnie. I'm so glad Ava's profession didn't scare you away."

Did he miss something? They hadn't been talking about her profession. Ahh. He mentally clapped his forehead. Lorna meant Ava's earlier *declaration*.

"Most men run for the hills when she tells."

Ava'd told other men she was a space creature? Who were these men and how did Lorna know about them? Arnie'd never kidded himself about being Ava's first victim, but it still rankled that Lorna would be crass enough to throw her previous conquests in his face. "I suggest I'm not most men," he grumbled.

"No. You certainly aren't," Lorna pinched his cheek, getting up to hop onto Gage's lap.

Her action left three people sitting and Ava standing. Arnie'd have to be a complete heel not to pat his lap. He threw in a smile for good measure.

When she settled down with a delicate squirm and sigh of contentment, Saturn Five aimed for glory. Maybe a little cosmic canoodling wasn't out of the question, after all. Arnie nuzzled her throat, loving the feel of that hair over his face, the mossy scent of her skin.

Her arms slithered round his neck and she pressed cool kisses along his forehead. He gazed up into bright green eyes and gave his head a mental shake.

What a way to go.

\* \* \* \* \*

*I'm in heaven*, Ava thought, unable to keep her hands from wandering all over Arnie. The night had grown cool, but his body gave off a preternatural heat she cocooned into, feeling safe and warm and cherished.

Her career didn't faze him. He hadn't even batted an eye. Her heart seized at the prospect that this might truly be the start of something enduring and grand.

He was brilliant, thoughtful and sensible. From that kiss in the kitchen, she knew him to be sensual and passionate beyond her wildest imaginings. All this and more rolled into one tasty hard-bodied package.

Some time ago, Gage had lit a fire in the BBQ pit. They lazed around a while before Lorna and Ava wandered inside for marshmallows. They were roasting the spongy buggers on a skewer when Arnie asked, "Do you work out of a hospital or do you have your own practice?"

Sitting at his feet, Ava checked her marshmallow. Too raw. She stuck it back in the fire and inhaled its sugary vanilla scent. "I'm a partner in a small practice. Someday, when Dr. Linus retires, I'll buy him out. Right now, though, I'm happy having a partner. Takes some of the heat off me."

"I suggest it does," Arnie said, fiddling with her hair. He couldn't seem to get enough of it, hadn't let go all evening. "What did you say your specialty was?"

Did he suffer memory lapses? Ava recalled their conversation before dinner and how he'd forgotten the topic. The realization distressed her and she wondered how much beer he'd consumed. Did he have a drinking problem? She opted for a jokey approach.

"Sheesh. We just talked about it a few minutes ago. You getting enough sleep?"

Arnie scowled. "We never talked about your specialty."

Gage and Lorna noticed the edge in his voice and tuned in to the conversation.

"Sure, we did." Lorna poked him in the ribs with a marshmallow stick. "Ava was thrilled you didn't mind. Remember?"

"Probabilism isn't a medical specialty," Arnie scoffed.

Ava's stomach somersaulted. *Oh no.* He'd misheard and thought she embraced the theory of uncertainty, which she did—otherwise she'd have answered the time question much differently. It was a logical assumption on his part, but this was bad. She didn't want him finding out this way.

Before she could warn the others, Gage shot back. "No, but proctology is and that's what we were talking about, cheesehead."

Ava wanted to burrow into the hedges. In the firelight, she watched the emotions play across Arnie's well-crafted features. There went confusion. Ah, wasn't that astonishment? She closed her eyes tightly against the next one on the docket, cracking a lid in time to see her worst fears coming to life on his face. Revulsion settled in for a nice long stay.

Dammit!

His bronzed gaze flamed over her like a blowtorch. "You're a proctologist?"

Ava cringed as he spat the word like a curse. No surprises there. But disappointment corkscrewed through her. He was just like all the rest.

She nodded.

"Aw shit!" Arnie bellowed, raking his face. "Shit!"

"That about sums it up," Gage said.

"I thought you explored galaxies, not gonads," Arnie roared, practically foaming at the mouth. He leapt to his feet, a wild look in his eyes.

"I do both," Ava said through aching teeth.

"Holy guacamole. How can you do that?"

"Somebody's got to."

"It's twelve squared!"

*He's calling it gross? That does it.* Ava scrambled up, poking a finger into his muscled chest. "You listen to me." She advanced as he retreated, stabbing over and over. "I'm sick and tired of people making fun of me. You think it's gross? How do you think I feel?" When he didn't answer, she narrowed her eyes. "*You* wake up one morning without an erection. You feel a strange evil beast coming to life in your body. You get diagnosed with prostate cancer and boohoo. Guess where you run? To me, buddy boy — the girl who does that *gross* thing."

"Bravo," Lorna cheered.

Ava turned and blew on her nails. "Thanks, girl." She spun back to Arnie. "Well?"

He was looking at her as if she'd taken a bath in pond scum. "I suggest it's a bit odd."

"You're a fine one to talk! Here you are with a degree from MIT and you're nothing but a glorified grease monkey. You should be using your education, making tons of money in a satisfying job."

"Is that what this is all about? Money?" He spat the word.

"No." Ava's chin lifted.

"Is that why you're a proctologist — for the money?"

"Never mind why I'm a proctologist." If she went into that now, she'd embarrass herself by crying. For all she knew, he'd laugh at the explanation like her neurosurgeon boyfriend in med school had — right before he dumped her. "I just am and you're going to have to deal with it."

Arnie rocked back on his heels and folded his arms across his chest. "And you'll have to deal with the fact that I'm a mechanic."

"That's different. I realized my potential, you threw away yours."

"So I'm supposed to maintain orbiters instead of aircraft."

"That's right."

He stiffened, sexy lips hardening into a tight white line. A tiny tic beat tattoos along his jaw. He seemed to hover for a moment, steeped in thought while his eyes roamed the sky, the yard, and finally, her face.

"You wouldn't want to be Spam in one of *my* cans."

She drew back. Did he doubt his abilities? "I heard NASA disagrees."

"Yeah and you know what NASA stands for?"

Gage groaned.

"Not Arnie Simpson's Arena."

"I don't believe that."

"Doesn't matter what you believe. That's the way it is. I'll never work for NASA."

"Maybe if you did, the space program wouldn't be in trouble."

A long, thick silence followed. She'd struck a nerve. When he finally spoke it was in a low, controlled voice.

"So now the disasters are my fault?"

"I'm just saying things might have been different."

"I'm not sure I'm supposed to feel good about that."

"Take it or leave it." Then, scared that he might actually leave it, she added. "It's a compliment but you should be aiming higher in your career." No way was he getting off easy. Now that they'd started down this road, might as well finish the journey.

"I could say the same about you."

The rejoinder came so quickly and smoothly it caught her off guard and she couldn't keep a smile at bay. Damn him for amusing her when she wanted to stay angry. "Touché."

Their eyes met and for a warm moment, understanding passed between them.

"I suggest we have a lot to learn about each other," he said seductively, niftily nipping her hostility. Awareness rippled through her. Before Arnie, all the other men who'd made fun of her career turned her off like a light switch. Why did he manage to melt her when the others couldn't?

*Stay on the subject. Just stay on the subject.* "I'd like to know why you're here when you should be there." Ava pointed to the sky.

"Ever since you landed, I'm glad I'm here."

*There was a subject*? She tossed her head and smiled and the silvering gleam in his eyes washed her whole body with infatuation. "That doesn't answer my question."

"Yeah, Arnie, why are you *here*?" Gage chimed in.

Arnie's eyes shut off and he threw Gage a poisonous look, making Ava wonder if this was an issue between the two men as well. Her curiosity swelled.

"What is this, an intervention?" Arnie joked, but she could see he was growing uncomfortable. After a moment, he turned to her, eyes large, soft and disturbingly vulnerable. "So we find each other's jobs distasteful. What would you suggest we do about it?"

"Fuggedabouit," Lorna said.

"I suggest she has a point."

"But you think what I do is gross."

"Who wouldn't?" he snorted, an emotion she couldn't ascertain flashing in his gaze.

"And I think what you do is wasteful. You should be out there making the world a safer, better place."

"Maybe I'm happy making *my* world a safer, better place," he countered.

"And I, for one, am grateful," Gage said. Lorna put a hand over his mouth.

"It's selfish. You have a responsibility."

"Look." Arnie put a hand at the base of her neck and started gently kneading. "Why don't we ditch these clowns, take a walk and talk about it."

His suggestion zipped straight through to her crotch and the message from his fingertips fanned out to parts she didn't even know she had. She swayed into the firmness of his body and he caught her close, his hard length arousing her beyond logic and reason.

She wasn't supposed to feel attracted to someone who couldn't understand her vision. While her mind screamed *Unfair!* her body told her life was full of injustice. Best to move along and enjoy it anyway.

Did she dare?

Breath hitching, Ava came to a decision. No matter the outcome of the conversation tonight, she intended taking advantage of the chemistry between them while she could. Opportunities like this—to literally explode in bed with someone—were far too rare to miss. Tomorrow would take care of itself. "Sounds like a good idea," she whispered, eyes glued to his.

"Rats. We always miss the good stuff," Gage complained through Lorna's fingers.

* * * * *

So she thought he could single-handedly rescue the space program. Arnie heaved a mental sigh. If she knew how far off the mark that impression was, she'd run hell for leather. Crap. He'd done a self-check on his intellect using the Apollo Thirteen disaster as a worst-case scenario, to see if he could solve the multitude of problems and bring the astronauts safely home. But the moron genes that ran in his family obviously didn't skip him entirely because he'd failed.

Had he been in the think tank those harrowing two days, everyone in the spacecraft would've died. So he'd concluded there was a black hole somewhere in his brain the size and general shape of the Sea of Tranquility. He was pretty good at most things, just not at the thing he wanted most.

"Let's go," he said and snatched her hand. He'd take her across the field to this little spot he knew—a natural spring that farted and belched continuously. She'd probably get a kick out of it.

He was glad they were leaving. Needed the break because she'd morphed from Pod Person to Prod Person before his brain fully acclimated to the former. Strolling beside her under the stars, he couldn't decide which incarnation was worse. He'd grown fond of the idea of an alien lover, although a proctologist lover wasn't all that different.

*Lover.*

She slid her hand down his back and tucked her slender fingers into his waistband. He could feel the soft, reptilian scratch of her fingernails. Would he ever get used to that sensation her touch caused on his skin—prickles of fire, like being caught in the middle of a meteor shower and living to tell. He grinned. Might not make it through this one.

"Are we going to talk, or not?" she said.

"Not," he said and twirled her around to face him. In the instant before her soft lips found his, all worries vaporized and scattered. She wiggled against his body, pressing those globes of pure desire against his chest, one long leg twining around his hips.

"I suggest there are other ways to solve our problems," he murmured into her mouth. If they could be solved. Talking wasn't going to change anything. Maybe they needed to communicate in a different way.

"As smart as we are, we ought to think of something," she said, tongue darting out to wet his upper lip. "What are you thinking right now?"

"I'm thinking this." He dropped his hand from her waist, slipped it through the slit in her skirt and took her pussy into his palm, rubbing until he felt her juices penetrating the thin nylon of her panties.

He wanted to drink her honey. To drop to his knees and bury his face inside the tent of her skirt. Her scent would blossom and surround him as her flavor sank into his tongue and into his bloodstream. Then *she* would pump through his system, nourishing him, making him grow, making him stronger than he thought he could be.

In a flash he crouched and yanked her over him. Bracing her legs with one arm, he slid inside the vee they formed and twisted until her pussy was centered over the top of his head. Then he lifted his face and planted his nose in her wetness, shoving the crotch of her panties aside and darting his tongue into her hot, waiting crevice.

She moaned and writhed at the assault. Her pussy clamped his tongue and made sucking noises as it spasmed. In the velvet stillness of night, her sounds hung in the air. He could pluck them and eat them like cherries off a tree. And they'd taste as sweetly tart. Because that's what he tasted right now as her fluids mingled with his and ran down his throat.

He gulped her, threading his tongue deeper inside and twirling for every last drop of her essence. Her labia cupped his nose, spreading and massaging her scent into his cheeks, enveloping him with Ava.

*Don't make me leave.*

"Oh God," she whispered. "Yes."

The sibilant sound vibrated along the bones of his face and funneled through his pipe works.

*We have ignition.*

Saturn Five's engines roared to life like a blast furnace. Only it was no longer Saturn Five. When had that changed? Now it was his cock roaring to life. Him roaring to life and aiming for the great unknown. Where would this ride take him? Would he ever return?

Too many questions to contemplate with his tongue buried in such a luscious cunt. He grinned against her slick flesh.

"I need something to hold on to," she gasped. "My balance is going."

He poked his head out of her perfumed tent and spotted a nearby tree, the perfect size for hanging. "We interrupt this program to bring you a special bulletin," he teased as he rose and scooped her up in his arms. A few long strides and they were underneath the nice smooth maple. Wouldn't do to rip the flesh off her back so early in the game. Unless she needed to shed.

He chuckled and she tossed him a skeptical look. He held her gaze as he unbuckled his belt and backed her up against the tree. "No escape." Wrapping the belt around her waist and looping it around the teenaged trunk, he buckled it loosely then stood back to admire his work.

"Not sure this is quite what I meant." Ava inspected her situation. Then she smiled. An impish gleam lit up her eyes and he dropped to his knees again.

Parting her skirt, he slid his hands along silken thighs. Her skin, baby soft and smooth, felt curiously hairless. No missed stubble. Just an unending velvet path.

He'd been too fucking horny to check out the color of her pubic hair. Now that he thought about it, there wasn't any. Seemed Miss Ava dared to go bare. Yeah. He liked that about her. But part of him yearned for curls that must surely be as warm and fine as cashmere.

Gently, he nibbled the tender flesh between her legs. She thrust her hips out and raised her arms to grab two branches, spreading herself wide open in a universally submissive posture.

Arnie took full advantage. With firm, kneading strokes he wiped his hands on her inner thighs, following up with his teeth to gently grind her soft skin in a biting massage. Her hips began to rotate with pleasure so he drew back for a moment to torture her.

"Lick me," she demanded.

He fanned his hands across her ass and lifted her legs onto his shoulders, angling her hips in front of his mouth and parting her fully. He let her hang, exposed in the cool air while he ran his thumbs around the rim of her portal and inspected every inch of her. Slowly, he slid the end of one thumb inside her cunt.

She mewed and flinched. Using both his thumbs, he tenderly widened her opening. Then with the tip of his tongue he teased at the luscious creamy frosting in the entrance.

She went ballistic, moaning and thrashing helplessly. *You've got her now.* Testosterone gushed through his system and he quickly undid the belt, forcing her to keep hanging on to the tree with her legs over his shoulders or slide down the trunk on her ass.

"Bastard," she half giggled.

*Move in for the kill.* Scrabbling with his lips in the darkness, he found her clit and pasted his tongue against it, pressing firmly and waggling with well-timed precision.

*Three, two, one. Blastoff!*

Jeez, he was glad he worked out. Her heels pummeled his back and he had to tighten her against his face to hold on. Sweet-tart syrup flooded his mouth, running down his chin. Nothing like an after-dinner drink! He swallowed and felt her energy power his blood.

What was that ungodly shriek? Good thing they were out in the country, though no doubt Lorna and Gage would hear. He laughed to himself while she shuddered.

She gasped and sputtered and sagged limply onto his shoulders. Afraid the branches might slip out of her weakened grip, he arranged her panties and started to swing her off one leg at a time.

Her thigh muscles tensed.

He glanced up at her.

She was staring out into the field, coiled, still and wary.

"Something wrong?"

"They're here."

The sac around his spine unzipped.

His brain said it could be a neighboring farmer, summoned by her cries, but his soul knew it wasn't. She knew it too.

"'S okay." He slid out from under her and stood up. She stumbled and leaned heavily on his flank.

"I'm scared." Turning those enormous green eyes to his, she nestled into the crook of his arm and placed a shaky hand on his pec. As if morbidly fascinated, she gazed back out into the night.

He heard her sniff.

Then her face lifted and she scanned the sky.

*She's looking for them.*

Heebie-jeebies staged a hoedown in his gut. What were the odds they'd have the same feelings? The same awareness of being watched? Part of him didn't want to ask. Didn't want to go there. But he had to. "Get this feeling often?"

Her head snapped around. "Once in a while."

Heebie-jeebies started slam dancing. He schooled his features and tightened his lips. "When?"

She chewed on her lower lip for several seconds before licking it and sucking in a breath. "When I'm on dates, actually." She snorted. "Maybe that's why it doesn't happen very often."

Like he believed that. Okay. He'd go with it for now. "Me too."

"Really?"

He nodded.

She fell silent for a moment. "It started when I hit puberty and after a while I noticed they would show up when I felt attracted to a boy."

Hoo boy. Now that she mentioned it…

"Do you think it's some psychosexual guilt?"

Arnie felt guilty about a lot of things. But never about sex. "Nah."

"Me either."

They stared at each other.

"I suggest it's probably nothing," he hedged. "Maybe just a desire that there actually be something else out there."

"Overactive imaginations," she eagerly agreed. Too eagerly. One last quick glance at the sky and a weird expression undulated across her face. Strange. He could've sworn it was rabid horniness, as if the thought of being observed turned her on.

She beamed at him, sliding her arms around his waist and tugging him in close. "You were incredible. I forgot to say that. Thank you."

Maybe it did turn her on. The exact opposite of what it normally did to him. Not tonight though. Tonight he felt remarkably cavalier. "You're welcome." On cue, the throbbing in his dick overwhelmed the throbbing in his stomach. Her lithe, slender form fit so perfectly with his body.

He liked her height, being able to look directly into her eyes without getting a crick in his neck. And the pounding of her heart next to his provided a sensual affirmation of life he'd never experienced before.

"Your turn, I think," she cooed and her hands slithered down to his hips.

He grinned. Fuck the *Observers*. Let Ava give 'em an eyeful.

Long, graceful fingers fluttered under his shirt and fiddled with the button on his khakis. She dipped that beautiful head of hair under his chin and tilted it, tickling his neck with her teeth and tongue. His skin tingled and his cock swelled painfully against the confining fabric of his pants as she licked up the side of his neck. Hot breath panted into his ear. She undid the button and the metallic sound of a zipper opening grew disproportionately loud and clanged with joyous anticipation in his brain.

Serpentine fingers embraced his member through his briefs as his pants puddled around his feet. Gently scrabbling, she discovered the portal and the skin-on-skin contact nearly drove him over the edge. If she could do this with fingers, what might she do with that mouth?

He grasped either side of her head for purchase and wound his fingers through corn silk hair. Her delicate, woodsy scent wafted into his nostrils and she began the journey down. Down.

Holy fucking shit.

Ava didn't mess around.

He convulsed as she sucked him into her tight, slick mouth and he felt her tongue bind the length of his shaft. Up. Down. His head found heaven at the back of her throat.

With incredible expertise and mind-boggling economy of movement she explored every sensitive region on his cock, fondled his balls gently in her hands, and generally proved how freaking awesome it was to be blown by someone who'd gotten a degree in men's anatomy.

Why hadn't he dated a proctologist before?

Every man should, at least once.

Like once would be enough.

His neck unhinged and his head fell back as he gulped wind just to stay on his feet. Overhead the stars started swirling, shooting fire across his eyes and raining down on his skin as molten energy surged into his cock. Then his body exploded and his liquids spurted into her mouth with the force of blood from a severed artery. Yet she kept going. Devouring, drinking her fill of him, absorbing every last drop of his life essence until he virtually sagged on the altar of submission.

Ava wiped her mouth on his briefs and politely pulled his pants up while the aftershocks rocked and rolled. Like a trooper, she said nothing, but cuddled into his shaky arms and stood holding him with her forehead brushing his.

"That was…" That was *what*? Earth-shattering, mind-altering, really, really neato? Somehow words didn't seem quite adequate. "Nice," he stammered lamely.

She giggled. "You're delicious."

"So are you." The echo of her flavor on his taste buds turned his blood to hot lava again. "I really want to fuck you," he blurted. Then cringed. He rarely spoke to a woman that way. Certainly not one he'd met yesterday. But then, what was typical about this relationship? Nothing he could see.

"I'd like that," she said. "Make it hard, fast and sweaty, please."

He could do that. In about thirty minutes from now. *They'd* time him. "Your wish is my command."

*To hell with Them. Go for it.*

But not here. He needed to buy some time. "This isn't the best place. Kind of scratchy."

Through the darkness her eyes shined into his. "Take me home?"

He had to stop and swallow the filthy talk puddling in his mouth. "Mine or Gage's?"

"What do you think?"

He gazed at this woman standing in front of him, tender lips pulled back in a smile, white teeth glistening with lubrication he'd provided, and affection socked him.

He liked her. "I suggest we go back for the car and thank Gage and Lorna."

He liked how she thought, how she looked, how she moved and how she moved him.

Normally, he didn't really like people. If he had to be honest, he'd say most were too dopey, and hence, too much trouble to deal with. But not Ava. She made trouble worth his while.

Hell, the way she looked now, tousled and flushed from their romp, he wouldn't have cared if she did turn out to be a space creature. In fact, too bad she didn't, because now that the afterglow had dissipated somewhat he decided what she did instead was twelve squared. Would he get used to it? Did he want to?

As if a meeting of the minds occurred somewhere out *there*, she nuzzled his shoulder and said, "Are you still grossed out by me being a proctologist?"

Could he answer safely? "I suggest I'm getting used to it." He grabbed her hand and started walking back to Gage's.

"It bothers you."

"Is that a problem?"

"You're not answering the question."

The trouble with a smart woman was she noticed small details like that.

"I mean," she continued, "even if it bothers you, we can still have fun this week."

Arnie froze in his tracks and turned to stare at her. "Is that how you see what's happened between us? As something *fun* for the week?"

She twisted her hand in his. "I'm not sure. I mean, I really like you…"

"I like you too."

"Then, fine."

"Okay."

"Okay."

They started walking again. What had he just agreed to? Searching the hidden files was a risky procedure. He stopped again. "Are you telling me we can fuck each other senseless tonight, but as long as I think proctology is gross there's no future for us?"

"Well." She drew a deep breath, swelling those heavenly breasts and eliciting an equal reaction from Saturn Five. "Isn't it important we support each other in what we do? I don't think I could tolerate a long-term arrangement otherwise."

Could he tolerate one knowing she had no respect for *his* job? "I see your point." But he did have respect for her job, just not the particulars involved. Then it hit him. She didn't see *him* as long-term material.

She saw him as a fling! Just when he was starting to see her as more. To hope for more. To *crave* more.

Part of his ego sailed over the moon. He'd never been anyone's boy toy before. But the other part flamed out on reentry. As appealing as the idea of no-strings-attached sex was, it wasn't what he wanted with her.

"So we agree. Party this week, then see what happens."

*What happens is I fall in love and you leave because I'm nothing but a glorified grease monkey.* "Don't know. I don't go for flings."

"Why not?" She met his eyes stridently. "We're free and over twenty-one. We've got great chemistry."

"But no respect."

Her head reared back, eyes shimmering. For some reason, she looked as if he'd slapped her.

"No," she whispered. "No respect."

Why did she sound teary? He was the one who should be bawling. He'd never encountered anyone who didn't respect him. Never. Yet she blew in from Metropolis and immediately held him to her city standard. Yet another reason to stay out of the armpits of the world.

"I suggest the outcome would not be good given our true feelings about each other," he finally said. Now he was sure he'd blown an O-ring in Lorna's kitchen.

"I'll find my own way home," she choked.

"It's just through those trees. I need to get the Sky-Watcher anyway." *And what's left of my gray matter.*

By the time they got there his heart was in retrograde. Nice way to end an evening of gourmet oral sex. He tossed around for something, anything, to make it less than disastrous. "I thought for a while we had something," he said, voice so low, so raspy it grated through his throat like sandpaper. "Especially by the tree."

Ava lifted her chin, folding her hands at the waist like a schoolmarm. "I guess we both got fooled."

"So you don't think there's any hope?"

"Not if we don't have respect."

He let loose an angry snort.

"It would never work anyway. We live worlds apart."

"In more ways than one."

Ava held out a shaky hand. "Nice meeting you, Arnold M. Simpson. See you at the rehearsal dinner."

Arnie ignored her hand, stalking to the telescope, tucking its massive weight under his arm and sauntering to the Porsche. Without another word he hopped in, fired the engine and gunned home.

Swerving into his driveway and skidding to a stop, he prayed for deliverance from this nightmare. Here he was, drooling all over his nice new shirt, considering interspecies marriage, actually believing he might be falling in love for the first time and she just saw him as an irresponsible boy toy.

His chest caved in. Here he'd fooled himself into thinking his intelligence attracted her, and she was more concerned with his worldly status. How smart could she be if she didn't see he was more than a mechanic? Had to be a mental midget, after all.

The thought saddened him so much he went inside and flopped down in bed fully clothed. Way down deep she was shallow. He supposed he was lucky to have found out early, before he'd invested too much of his nonexistent time.

# CHAPTER FIVE

"He has no respect for me, Lorna, he said so right to my face." *After I blew his head off.* Ava stuffed the pillow she'd been leaning on into a wad around her stomach and reached for her wine.

"I don't believe it. Arnie's not that shallow."

"I guess you don't know him as well as you think."

Lorna chewed her lip, concern folding her normally serene brow. "He'll come around. He's in shock."

"Yeah, well, guess what? I don't want him to come around. The tone of his voice did me in. I can't get past the disgust anymore. It makes me sad and I won't tolerate it."

Though Lorna and Gage had made themselves scarce during the final round in the backyard, they'd been well aware of what had happened. Gage had preceded the women to bed after apologizing profusely. He felt terrible but it wasn't his fault.

"You misunderstood," Lorna said, almost as miserable as Ava.

"There was no misunderstanding," Ava snarled, patting Lorna's hand to take the sting out. "Look. This is your wedding. You should be happy. *We* should be happy. Let's forget about this whole rigmarole and move on. Tell me about the cake."

Gratefully, Lorna took the hint and began a detailed description. While she droned, Ava tried paying attention, but her thoughts kept straying to those last moments with Arnie.

It was about time she stood up for herself instead of slinking into a hole, trying to hide from male derision. She took an incredible sense of pride in how she'd backed him into a corner with outrage and made up for all the times she'd yearned to do that but hadn't. What confused her was this feeling of doom that clung to her heart like cobwebs. Why did it have to be Arnie?

It irked her royally that he reacted like the rest. She wanted so badly for him to be different, to want her enough to accept and respect her for who she was. But he hadn't, dammit. And wasn't that the straw that broke her back.

Here was a man, ideal in every way save one and she couldn't tempt him to have a mere fling with her, let alone a relationship. She had the same bad luck with the best as she had with the worst. What was wrong with the world? With proctology? With her?

If her father could see her now, he'd laugh hysterically. *Thanks, Dad.* She'd done this for him and look what she got. No chance for children of her own. No chance to follow in his footsteps and break their hearts by dying young. No chance to enjoy creating them in the first place.

Sonofabitch!

"Even though Gage thinks calla lilies are for funerals, I still ordered them," Lorna giggled. "Ava? Are you listening?"

"What? Oh. Tell him to go stuff it."

Lorna sighed, grabbing Ava's hands and squeezing them. "Don't get bitter, please. I couldn't stand it if you did."

Hot tears pricked Ava's eyes and she pulled a hand free to swipe at them. "Easy for you to say. Gage is gaga over you."

"And Arnie's into you." At Ava's skeptical look, she continued. "I've never seen him like this. Honestly. With his last girlfriend, he was polite, treated her nicely but you could tell she didn't captivate him. Of course, no one's smart enough to challenge him, to arouse his passion and that's where you come in. Gage and I were floored by that kiss in the kitchen. And those howls from the field. Arnie doesn't do stuff like that. He'll. Be. Back."

"Nice speech, but Lorna, I don't want to see mugging across the breakfast table every morning when it's time to go to work. How would you feel if Gage rolled his eyes and made puking sounds every time you sat down to write a column?"

Lorna drew back, surprised. "Arnie did not make a puking noise."

"Might as well have."

Lorna thought for a moment before saying, "I'd hate it." She hugged Ava. "I never looked at it that way before. Oh honey."

Before she could stop them, the floodgates opened and Ava started bawling.

* * * * *

When she awoke the next day, a puffy face said howdy-do from the mirror. Great. She wanted to kick something. Tonight was the rehearsal and dinner party afterward. She wanted to look smashing, to rub Arnie's nose in what he was missing. But the bags under her eyes and that swollen glob of fat under her chin mocked her wishes.

Hollering down the hall for an ice pack, she narrowed her eyes at her reflection. Darned if he'd know she'd been crying.

A long, hot shower and artfully applied makeup boosted the effects of the ice, reassuring her that by tonight, she'd be back to normal. Rooting through the makeup kit in her bedroom, she noticed she'd left one of her essential beauty potions behind in Minneapolis. It was probably hopeless to search for it in Podunk, but she needed some downtime anyway.

With this in mind, she meandered into the kitchen to find Gage alone at the table.

"Coffee's in the pot, toast is in the oven," he said, glancing up from the newspaper.

She waved the offer aside. "I need to go shopping and figured I'd test the fare at your greasy spoon. Where's Lorna?"

"Showering."

Ava nodded, adjusting the purse strap on her shoulder. "I'm going to wander around. Need to think. Will you tell her?"

Gage looked apologetic again so Ava held up both hands. He got the hint.

"I'm flying to Madison after lunch to get Lorna's folks," he said. "If you're busy, I'll take Lorna with."

Ava saw he really wanted Lorna's company and her heart sank. No one wanted *her* company. But she pasted on a semblance of a smile and said, "Great. Take her. Just get home in time for the rehearsal."

"Sure thing, Mom," Gage grinned. "I'll leave the back door open. Ever since Miss City Girl took up residence, I'm supposed to lock it. Don't rat me out."

Ava shook her head, remembering those long-ago days when locks weren't even installed on her family's door. "Sure thing, Captain. See ya."

Minutes later she stepped inside Flintlock's only diner. Whoa! The whole town seemed to be here, packing the booths, spilling into the aisles.

Off to one side, farmers were settling in for a morning jaw. One group so huge it had pushed three tables together caught her attention.

A half-dozen gigantic men wearing overalls and John Deere caps guffawed. Three or four heavily pregnant women, faces scarlet, tried to hide smiles behind menus so as not to egg the men on. And perched silently at the end of the table sat Arnie.

Ava ducked behind a skinny palm. Slumped in the chair, one leg out as if to make a quick getaway and eyes wandering, he was the very picture of boredom. While she watched, he picked lackadaisically at breakfast, took a sip of coffee, checked his chronograph. One of the pregnant women poked him in the ribs and he sent her a faint smile. His sisters? But who were the men? Couldn't be his brothers. No way. Yet Lorna'd claimed they were polar opposites. Ava hadn't guessed she meant physically.

These men were circus freaks. Not one of them under six-two. If Arnie hadn't been alone at the end of the table, they would've swallowed him up with their mass. And they were blond — those who had hair.

Probably neighbors.

Glancing left, she spotted an open seat at the counter. It had a clear view of Arnie's table, but if she held the obscenely large menu in front of her face, he'd never be the wiser.

A quarter of an hour later, she dug into a farm-fresh meal. *They sure grew them eggs big around here*, she thought. *And will you take a look at those rashers*. She wondered idly if it was a Simpson hog she was chewing when a tap came on her shoulder.

She whirled to see a grim-faced Arnie.

"Why didn't you come over and say hello?"

Ava tried acting casual but her face heated. "I didn't see you." She didn't want to admit she liked watching him when he was unaware. Only, it turned out he'd been aware all along. Damn that sixth sense.

A brief flash burned in his eyes. "I suggest that palm isn't big enough to hide me, let alone you."

"I didn't want to interrupt," she countered lamely.

"Is that all?"

"Arnie, we said our piece last night. What do you want from me?"

Something flared on his face and he flinched. "Nothing," he finally said. "I thought we could be polite — especially after spit-shining each other with our tongues. But I suggest that's asking too much."

He stared daggers at her while she struggled for words, then he spun on his heel and burst out the door.

"Arnie!" Ava threw a wad of bills on the counter and charged out to the street. Empty, like a town awaiting a pistol duel.

*Curse you, Arnie Simpson*!

Glancing west, she saw dust billowing along the airport road. She considered hoofing out there to harangue him and while she hung in indecision, feeling like a skunk, the behemoths lumbered out onto the sidewalk.

"What happened to the runt?" one of them roared.

Ava shot the horizon with her finger. "He went thataway."

"Thanks, ma'am." The biggest one tipped his hat, doing a double take when he spied her hair. "Hey, aren't you Lorna's maid of honor?"

"That's me," Ava said, extending a hand. "Ava Ward."

"Tiny Simpson." He buried her hand in his paw and started pumping, answering her question without her having to ask. "The wedding's going to be a humdinger."

"So I've been told," Ava said, softening her tone with a smile.

"Hey, let me introduce you." Tiny gathered the others into a tight circle and started handing out names. Ava's head spun when he was done. "But we'll be seeing you tonight, anyway, at the rehearsal." Tiny squinted into the horizon. "So the squirt hightailed it off to work, eh?"

"Looks that way," Ava said.

"I'll never figure him out. Smart as a whip, but doesn't know what he wants."

Ava perked up. "No?" Maybe Tiny agreed Arnie should be using his education.

Tiny shook his head. "Ordered a three-egg omelet this morning and hardly took a bite. Isn't that right, Marty?"

One of the others nodded.

"Wasted all that good food."

Ava let out the breath she'd been saving. Wow. Lorna was right. Arnie really was the changeling of the Simpson clan.

*Changeling.*

Her skin frosted over. Could it be? Had he been adopted? Lorna had indicated otherwise, but it would certainly explain why he was so different. She turned back toward the airport, as if the dust he'd left in his wake held the secret.

*Who are you? What do you want?*

Had he ever questioned his pedigree? What if his mother had an affair? Or his father, for that matter? What if neither of them were his parents? What if no one in this town, or no one on this Earth…

She shook her head.

Too much astrobiology on the brain. While she firmly believed in other life forms, she wasn't buying the "evidence" that they'd already landed. Phenomena existed, and perhaps they were circling, but in the end, she'd believe it when she'd seen it rather than felt it.

And yet, Arnie's mind reading, his intelligence, those mood eyes… She chewed her lip thoughtfully as the Simpsons shook hands all around, said so long and headed off to work. Then she headed off too. And shooed him from her mind.

It didn't matter. He didn't matter. Once the wedding was over she'd be back in her world. And Arnie had no place in it. No place at all.

Now if only that accursed lump in her throat would smooth out.

By the time she'd checked out every shop along the two-block length of Flintlock, had a root beer float at the soda fountain in the Emporium and watched a double matinee at the State Theatre, the afternoon waned into early evening.

She hadn't wanted to risk running into Arnie again so she'd stayed off the streets and out of the sun. Now, as she emerged from the theatre, she felt disoriented from being in the dark so long. The bright sunshine had vanished and ominous charcoal clouds boiled overhead. An eerie quiet had descended on the town. Glancing skyward, she figured with luck she could make it back home before the rain.

As she jogged along the sidewalk the first fat splashes of the summer thunderstorm hit her arm. A burst of primal excitement nipped her heels as the earthy, electrical scent of rain teased her nostrils and the first crack of thunder shook the sky.

Lifting her hand to shield her eyes from the drops, she paused to absorb the majesty of the lightning display over distant, rolling farms. A writhing wall of rain advanced from the west like a monochromatic aurora as the front moved in. Ava stood in awe of its quick progress across the pastures, down Main Street, to a final collision with her.

Face raised, lips parted, she opened her arms in sheer ecstasy as the rain wrapped around her like a sheet.

* * * * *

Arnie was cursing and spewing over the mechanical failure du jour when the phone shrilled inside the hangar office. He automatically checked the clock as he jogged inside to answer, making note of the time on a pink message pad while picking up the receiver. Five o'clock. Two hours until the torture of seeing Ava would begin.

"Flintlock Municipal," he barked.

"It's Gage," came the disembodied, crackly voice.

"Got a bad connection."

"I need your help."

Arnie felt a stab of concern. "Shoot."

"Lorna and I are in Madison. Airport's closed. Bad storms."

"Okay, I'll cancel the rehearsal."

"Wait! We can't get a hold of Ava. Lorna's worried she got locked out—"

The line went dead.

*Shit.* Arnie slammed down the phone, threw his tools in the box, backpedaled to count them and hopped into his pristine Porsche without changing clothes.

The rain had let up but the temperature had dropped by a good thirty degrees. He coaxed the antique car down the muddy, rutted road, dodging meteor-sized hailstones and cussing up a storm.

When the tires finally found pavement, he put pedal to metal and roared toward Gage's house on the other side of town. As he shot down Main, he kept an eye peeled for Ava. All the storefronts were darkened, the awnings retracted. Passing the gas station, he figured out why. Power was out. The emergency generators at the airport must have kicked in without him noticing. He'd had his mind on Ava instead of on the weather, where it should've been.

*Asshole.*

Screeching to a halt in front of Gage's, he sprang out of the car. A fine mist of drizzle interspersed with fat drops from the tree branches blotched his T-shirt as he bounded up the stoop and pounded on the front door.

"Ava," he bellowed. "Avaaaaa."

"Arnie?" a tiny voice chattered from under the cherry tree to his right.

He peered at the tree. Its weeping bows, heavy with water-laden leaves, hung in a closed drape around a circular bench. He crunched through the hail, parted the branches and found her huddled in a ball, blue-lipped and quivering, white hair hanging in clumps like a drowned kitten.

There was blood on her forehead. Red blood. Except for some weird little dark flecks.

Must be dirt.

"Ava," he whispered, gathering her in his arms. She trembled so violently he could hardly contain her. "You're bleeding." He eyeballed her forehead and saw the thin trail of speckled blood led up to a goose egg near her part. She must've gotten nailed by the hail. But she'd live. "Locked out?"

She nodded spastically.

"Let's get you fixed up." Gingerly, he pulled her to her feet, keeping his arm tight around her slim waist as he escorted her to the car. "How long you been out here?"

She tried to talk but finally gave up with a sheepish smile and a shrug. His heart flip-flopped wildly. Now that she was safe, all the disaster scenarios he'd rejected during the brief search stampeded into his brain.

What if she'd been knocked out by the hail, or struck by lightning? It'd happened before around here, not long ago. Something deep inside him curled up at the thought of her alone and in pain. Or dead.

*Forget it, sphincter. She's not yours to worry about.*

But his heart refused to listen. Instead, it exploded in his rib cage when she raised trembling eyebrows and tittered. She was on the verge of hypothermia yet still managed to find humor in her predicament. He turned the heater on full blast. It'd barely gotten lukewarm by the time he pulled into his driveway. *Some help you are, moron. Now's your big chance. Don't blow it again.*

He herded her inside to the bathroom, sat her down on the toilet and unscrewed the knobs on the bath. While it filled, he kneeled in front of her and started prying her arms apart. "It's okay. Let go." She was stiff as a board and shaking so violently he imagined her skeleton rattling. He clucked soothingly, massaging tight muscles until they began to relax.

Finally, she lunged forward and wrapped her arms desperately around his neck. He backed his face out of damp, meadow-scented hair and stood them both upright. Frightened eyes met his and clung. "Ava," he rasped.

Her blue lips looked like ripe Concord grapes. He was a shithead for taking advantage like this but before he knew it he was nibbling, tasting, sampling that sweet, warm mouth that held him and Saturn Five captive the night before.

And how sweet it was. His hands glided along her slender frame, finding those soft, warm places he'd become addicted to. Her firm ass revolved erotically when he molded both hands around it, docking her neatly with his swelling cock.

Writhing against him, she brushed hardened nipples across his chest. A feral growl rose up from his gut. She quaked in his arms. He pulled her tighter and lost control.

Steam billowed out from the bathwater, filling the room and surrounding them in a cocoon of heat and moist passion. He imagined they looked like one solid tangled lump of flesh to the *Observers*.

And didn't give a flying fuck.

He could make love to her anytime, anywhere. Alone or in mixed company. Because when she was around his brain had no space for anything else. Ava filled him. Completed him. Owned him.

He was such a flippin' goner he couldn't fight it anymore.

Yet he had to. She needed him to.

Blood pounded in his ears, Saturn Five on the verge of burning up. With an inner strength he didn't want to possess, he lassoed his senses and unwound her arms. The urgent care she needed took precedence over the burgeoning fireball in his pants.

"Can you get undressed?" he asked, eyeing those glued-on jeans.

Obediently, her frozen fingers fumbled at the button, her teeth clattering more by the minute. With an exasperated groan, he hoisted her up by the waist, spun her around back to chest, and climbed into the tub. Work boots and all.

He had no idea how, but he got them submerged in the hot water. Her soft curves spooned against him as she shivered and purred with pleasure.

"Th-this h-happened once in F-fairbanks," she said. "My parents put me in the tub t-too."

"When did you visit Alaska?" he asked, to make conversation and keep her mind busy. He realized he knew next to nothing about her family. He'd been too busy wondering which world she'd come from to wonder where she'd been in this one.

"I grew up…grew up…" she mewed, succumbing to a final, body-wrenching chill.

"You grew up in Fairbanks?"

She nodded.

*Better visibility way up there…a vacuum…*

What a blockhead.

*Outer space, if you ask me…*

His jaw locked. She was an Alaskan, not an alien!

While they lay wedged intimately together, all the metaphors he'd used to describe her blew a ragged hole in his brain, leaving a window on how he'd distanced himself by imagining she was a Visitor. This phenomenal body, pressed trustingly into his, belonged to the most completely, joyfully *human* being he'd ever touched and who'd ever touched him.

And those slender fingers touched Uranus for a living.

He had to get out of here. "Finish your bath," he ordered, sliding out from under her and rising in a slosh. "I'll make you something to eat."

"Arnie?"

He stopped and turned.

"Thanks for coming to find me."

He snapped a salute, dropped a towel over the puddle he'd made and dove for cover. Streaking up to the bedroom, he slammed and locked the door, checking it twice before peeling off his clothes.

It took about an hour and a half just to get out of the wet jeans, but he finally piled all his togs in a soggy heap on the floor. He took a moment to wonder how Ava was faring with her clothes then abruptly shuttered his mind to the picture of her naked, like Venus rising, only a blink away.

*A robe, a robe, my kingdom for a robe.* He rooted through the black hole of his closet, emerging with a brand spanking new silk bathrobe Nora had bought him as a gag gift one Christmas. He found scissors and snipped off the tag.

After making himself decent in allegedly clean sweatpants and a familiar old AirGage tee, he crumpled the robe into a ball, took a deep, shaky breath, and headed for the bathroom.

She was singing in the tub.

Holy hot flashes, how much was one man expected to take? Rapping a warning, he cracked the door and tossed the robe inside. There. He'd done something rational. Now he needed to make dinner.

His nerves played jingle bells as he threw frozen steaks under the broiler, washed fresh greens and tossed two potatoes in the nuclear power plant.

Remembering his promise to cancel the rehearsal, he got on the horn to set up a phone chain and neatened his pad. A quick surveillance of his scant possessions spiraled him into fresh panic. The furniture was hideous. How had that gone unnoticed all these years? And the dust! He yanked the T-shirt over his head and swiped manically. Coughing, he stepped back for inspection.

The drain stopper popped. Water gurgled ominously through the pipes. He bolted upstairs for a clean shirt.

By the time she emerged, hair in a towel, skin flushed and dewy, dinner sat steaming on the table and Arnie had struck a relaxed pose against the kitchen sink. "Better?"

One glance at her, wrapped up in his robe like Christmas in July, was enough to start terminal countdown all over again. Would he ever get a break?

"Much. Oh, Arnie, this looks delicious."

Her grateful smile sent him into orbit. Head whirling like a turbine, he pulled out a chair, felt the delectable weight of her ass hit the seat, and pushed the chair back in.

"Aren't you eating too?"

He nodded, grabbing a plate and sitting down across from her. With a pop, he uncorked the red wine, filled two glasses and handed her one. Her appreciative coos when she bit into his meat echoed through his cock in orgiastic revelation. That's how she'd sound arching under him, moaning, squeezing the essence from his soul.

With a clobber to the head and heart he was too lame to anticipate, Arnie knew he'd fallen hopelessly in love.

"That was amazing," she whispered, leaning back in satiation. Her intelligent green eyes settled on his, seeming to search for an answer he was too dumb to give.

"Feeling better?" he repeated when his dependable mind failed again.

She nodded, taking a sip of wine. "Much. Nice robe," she added, fingering the fine silk. "Doesn't seem like your style though."

He smiled. "Gag gift from my dorky sister. You can keep it if you want." *You can keep me too.*

"I might just do that," she purred. "Hey!" she leaned forward again, eyes alert. "Where are Gage and Lorna? They okay? What about the rehearsal?"

Arnie explained as he cleared away the dishes, reliving the rescue mission and scaring himself all over again with new and improved disaster scenarios.

"Lorna must have locked the door when they left," Ava mused, remembering Gage's warning. "I thought I was a goner."

"You should've called me," Arnie said then kicked himself. *With what, telepathy?*

"I almost walked to the airport but then it started hailing. I got whacked." She whipped the towel off her hair and felt around her scalp. "Yup, there's a goose egg."

Arnie reached out to touch the bump. "That's a doozy," he agreed, allowing his fingers another stroke before withdrawing. "You want a pill for it?"

"Nah." She got up, tightening her sash, snagging her goblet and heading for the sofa. "Nice digs," she said and curled up for a stay.

"Liar," he said. "It stinks."

The green eyes widened and hopped around. "Could use a woman's touch."

*So could I.*

"How come you have electricity? I saw a transformer get hit."

Arnie ambled over and sat next to her. "I hooked up emergency generators. See that?" He pointed to a small red light above the door. "Shows it's working."

Ava turned in amazement. "I did the same thing! For some reason my townhouse always loses power. Must be hooked up to the wrong grid. I got totally sick of that."

Arnie grinned, a heated, gooey sensation clogging his veins when their eyes met. "Playtime with the geeks," he said.

Ava quirked an eyebrow. "No such thing." She sounded bitter, he thought. "Sometimes I wish I could kick back and turn the old brain off. It's not in the cards, though."

"Nope," he agreed. "That's why you're so slim."

Ava laughed. "What?"

"The average brain burns twenty-five watts a second. I don't think there's a measurement for a bulb as bright as yours."

She scooted an inch closer. He cleared the giant hairball out of his throat, getting up because he felt loopy with desire. If he could just get over the love thing, he'd gladly take her up on the casual sex she'd offered last night—right here, right now—even though she wouldn't respect him in the morning.

But, since he doubted he'd ever get over the love thing, that meant he'd never get over her once he entered her pearly gate. For his own safety and the future of his personal space program, he had to leave now. "I've got a few dents to hammer out of the Porsche. Make yourself at home."

And he made himself scarce.

# CHAPTER SIX

The muffled rumble of a garage door scrolling reached Ava's ears, then the clank of tools and the speedster's roar as Arnie drove it in.

She remained on the couch, savoring her wine and giving him time to believe he made a clean getaway.

Miraculously, she'd been blessed with a second opportunity.

The lengths he'd gone to ensure her safety carved a notch in her heart. He'd actually climbed into the tub with her, for crying out loud! He'd made dinner, found her something to wear.

By no means an expert, she certainly had enough experience to know that a man with no respect for a woman wouldn't do things like that.

Arnie felt more deeply than he realized. She'd have to help bring his feelings to the surface. Make him consciously aware of what he felt for her and free him up to fuck her stupid. And maybe more.

In short, he needed a good swift kick in the ass. And damned if she wouldn't give him one. Because he was a keeper. Totally worth some extra effort on her end.

If her profession creeped him out, she'd make him understand why she chose it. Unlike the others, he was more than capable of comprehending the fear and loss that drove her into it.

A crisp freshness whirled through her. For the first time, she'd met a hero, a man worthy of her own respect and one who would protect her if she needed it. So why was she sitting like a glob of gelatin on the sofa?

Because he still might reject her. He had once already. What if he did it again? But he wouldn't. Her heart knew it. If only her heart would tell her brain.

Draining her wine with a giant gulp, she stood up and padded into the bathroom. The ghost-white face staring back from the mirror shocked the crap out of her. No wonder he'd run screaming.

*Get him back. Sic 'em!*

Straightening her shoulders, she finger-combed her hair, pinched color into her cheeks, and turned toward the garage.

Time to give Arnold M. Simpson a licking.

He had the passenger door panel off and was bent over tapping at dents when Ava approached. That fine, firm ass swung seductively with each rap, his thigh muscles tensing under the thin fabric of his sweats.

She noted the fibrous cords in his arms, the camel-backed curve of biceps and his hair slicked damply off his face, giving her a clear view of classic features — in all their sweaty glory.

Had she called him cute? This version wasn't cute at all. He had a finely chiseled face, determined and square jawed. And that body... Every feminine cell inside her saluted him. "How's it going?"

He wheeled around, banging his shin on the door. "Ah shit!"

"Sorry," she laughed. "Didn't mean to scare you."

He ran a hand through his hair, pushing it back farther on a high, intelligent forehead. "'S ok. Didn't expect you."

"Thought you might like some company," she offered softly.

His gaze swiveled and focused and his lips curled up in a predatory smile. "I'd like a lot of things I can't have."

"Me too." Ava smiled back and advanced a step, pouting and gesturing toward the car. "Imagine leaving this poor baby out in the storm. It has a beautiful body and you should take better care of it."

The embers in his eyes flickered and flared over her. "I suggest I should."

She slithered closer, sliding a hand along a mirrored fender. "I think you left it out on purpose so you could tinker on its voluptuous curves."

His grin deepened. Did he have those rakish dimples an hour ago? "I suggest I might've," he growled. His pupils had widened, lapping her up and glittering as the moods inside him evolved.

The heated blood in her veins thinned and rushed through her heart, making it wobble and thump with surging desire. She hadn't come out here for sex. She'd come out to talk. But the testosterone riding out on his breath clogged her thoughts until all she wanted to do was rip off her robe and wallow in it. "We need to talk," she whispered.

He stepped toward her with silvering eyes and once again she became ensnared in his tracking beam. "I suggest we've talked too much already. Time to shut up and make love."

"Oh Lord."

He ran the backs of his fingers down her cheek and a waterfall of tingles marked the trail. But he stopped abruptly when he reached her neck. "I'm filthy," he muttered and turned to grab a rag.

"That's okay." *Better seize the opportunity to be sensible.* "We need to talk. Really."

A shutter slammed and extinguished the beacon in his gaze. The sinuous strength in his body diminished as he pulled out of his pounce. For a moment, she was knocked off kilter. Before her eyes he transformed from sex-starved beast to innocuous country boy. Even his hair flopped down. "Talk about what?"

"Why I went into proctology."

He flinched. "You don't need to—"

"Yes. I do." Ava drew a tense breath and bore on. "When I was fourteen, my dad developed prostate cancer." Suddenly she teetered on the edge of the dark tunnel of time. Like a vacuum hose, it inhaled her, tugging her flesh, plucking her thoughts, pulling out emotions she preferred to keep closeted.

Arnie held up a hand, his expression grim. "I'm sorry—"

"No. I have to tell you." If she let him stop her now, she'd never venture in there again. She rested a hand on the car to steady herself and envisioned herself spread-eagled and holding on for dear life at the sucking mouth of the tunnel. "It took a long time for him to go. For a while he seemed fine. But..." Her fingers twisted into a pretzel. "It metastasized into his bones. Arnie, he'd sit at the kitchen table and weep. He was a powerful, vital man. But the cancer ate him from the inside out. He told me it felt like white-hot hooks were ripping the flesh from his bones. I held his hand when he died."

"When was that?"

"My sixteenth birthday."

Arnie barked out a harsh laugh. "Happy birthday, sweet sixteen."

"Tell me about it." She swiped at her eyes. "Anyway, I vowed never to let another father and child go through that hell. Not on my watch. And as disgusting as it might seem, that's why I do what I do."

They stared unflinchingly into each other. Arnie's jaw clenched once. Then with deliberation, he set down his tool. Quietly noting the remainders of grease on his hands, he moved to the sink and with agonizing thoroughness, soaped each finger. Shaking them off, he reached for a clean rag. One by one he dried them. Tossing the damp rag in a bin, he turned back to Ava and advanced.

His sable gaze was so intense, Ava swallowed and backed away until the corrugated tin wall of the garage fused with her spine.

Wordlessly, he kept coming.

"Well?" she hiccoughed.

He parked his hands on either side of her head, hemming her in an arm's length away. Staring into her face, his gaze caressed each feature.

Were stars exploding in his eyes? There was so much swirling action in those deep dark depths Ava couldn't pin down one stellar event for interpretation. It was the Big Bang all over again—she hoped.

Finally, his gaze landed on her lips. His head tilted to the right and he bent his elbows to lean closer.

Ava gasped. His warm breath provided her only caress. He didn't move his hands, didn't budge his body from a yard away. Only his eyes and wine-scented breath stroked her.

Then, at last, his mouth.

Ava groaned as his lips opened and fastened hungrily onto hers, tongue sprinting a lap around her mouth, shattering her and spewing her pieces into the far corners of space. A cathartic solar wind blew her heart wide open in bracing and grateful relief. As if they had a long history together, had been separated for a millennium, and were only now reunited.

Where that sense came from she didn't know and didn't care. All she knew was the sense of fellowship, of belonging, was powerful and secure. At this moment it seemed as if nothing could stand in its way.

At this moment…

The absence of touching heightened and magnified what his lips were doing. What they continued to do for an ungodly length of time. She'd never known a man to kiss this invasively.

With a low, impatient purr she arched into him, desperate for a more profound contact. He clasped her shoulders before she reached him and drove her insane with this unbearable distance. She mewed in protest. His lips unlatched.

"I suggest we go upstairs." He grabbed her hand and dragged her behind him, leading her to a doorway into the house and through the living room with a domineering sense of purpose that had her heart, and her pussy, pounding.

Never in a geologic epoch would she have guessed a rocket-nerd could be such a sexual Tasmanian devil. The way he'd ravaged her inside out last night, the way he commandeered her physically and emotionally tonight…

As a doctor she'd always been the one in control. Always needed to be. It shocked the shit out of her that submission to his raging desires made her so freaking horny. That sturdy, agile body sent her to her knees with a wailing, desperate plea.

She stopped in her tracks. Wanted his eyes on her again. Wanted him to praise her beauty and worship her the way she was idolizing him right now.

She jerked her hand out of his, causing him to turn abruptly to face her. In one graceful movement she shimmied the robe off her shoulders like a stole. Her hair cascaded down her bare back and settled around her face. "Arnie," she whispered. "Look at me."

He didn't seem to notice her naked breasts. Instead he locked on to her eyes and plunged inside her mind. Could she climax from eye contact alone? The ear-splitting squeal of her clit said *yeah, baby*.

She squirmed beneath his scrutiny and a cold blade of fear teased her sternum. What if he didn't like what he saw? She'd never been this insecure before.

"I *am* looking at you."

Yes. He was.

For the first time she was being seen—thoroughly seen—for the woman she'd become.

Adrenaline released a rebel yell that reverberated down to her toes.

He moved closer, tightening his visual chains.

She lifted her chin. "Now touch me." Her voice clattered clumsily in her throat and she had to remind herself she was an accomplished, professional woman. Not a pimply girl begging the cool boy to like her.

With an animal sound, he yanked her against his hard length and his mouth clamped over hers. If two people could eat each other, this is what it'd feel like, she thought as his lips trammeled hers, sucking, nibbling, leaving his scent on her skin to thread into her nostrils and lash her mind to the stake.

Her hands grazed the expanse of his back, finding the smooth, sculpted valley along the river of spine and floating blissfully down. His muscles tensed and released as his own desperate hands explored her.

Work-roughened palms licked and snagged her flesh like a cat's tongue, a sensation so unique and purely male her core boiled over and liquid oozed onto her thighs.

Frantically, she plucked at his shirt bottom, sliding her fingers along the solid ridges of his stomach. Wind whistled through his teeth as she fiddled with his waistband, his abs coiling beneath her trembling hands, his cock straining the elastic like a battering ram.

"Ava," he rasped. His fingers tangled with her hair and he plunged his face into its still-damp strands. She had him gloriously naked in a wink—that tan, hard body poised before her like a Greek god.

"Oh," she panted at his flawless male beauty.

"I suggest it's your turn." His voice smoldered, singeing a fire line down her backbone to the lusty control center between her legs.

"I'm halfway there, and you didn't even notice," she teased, half afraid he had but wasn't impressed.

"You don't think so?" he asked softly, capturing her face in powerful hands and smoothing her hair away. His lips fluttered on her forehead, down her nose, across her cheeks and eyelashes. Blazing a sensual trail, his fingers danced along her neck, circling her shoulders and chest before gently molding her breasts. "You're unreal," he murmured, worshipping her with each touch. "I don't need to see this," he twirled one nipple between his thumb and index fingers, "or taste this," he bent his head and suckled the other, "to want you more than I've ever wanted anyone."

"Oh Arnie," she choked.

"But," he lifted his face and smiled wolfishly, "having seen them, I suggest I wouldn't kick you out of bed."

Ava giggled, then grew serious, running her hands along broad shoulders, enamored with the fact that minus his work boots, he stood eye to eye with her. "It's important to me that you think I'm beautiful, physically, I mean. I know that sounds shallow…"

"Ava." He pressed a thumb against her lips and slipped the tip inside for a nibble. "Bite me." Then he swept her up in his arms and bounded up the stairs.

With a grace won from years of physical labor, he angled through the narrow hallway, carried her to his bed and reverently spread her out. Kneeling on the mattress beside her, he watched her face as he slowly slid his hand down her stomach to untie the sash on her robe. Ava's eyes rolled back at the pleasure of his nimble fingers on her heated skin, the anticipation of them moving lower.

With his right hand, he parted the robe along the outside of her thighs while the other hand roamed up the inside. Like a magician, he waved it palm down over her bald mound before gently cupping and kneading. "What color is your pussy hair?"

"Dark. I waxed for the summer. You like?"

"Yeah. But let it grow."

He crouched over her and her legs fell open as he caressed her, parting her labia and slipping a fingertip across the engorged, sensitized nub of her clitoris. As if gingerly coaxing a nut from a bolt, he expertly took her apart with his thumb and forefinger.

Ava yelped his name and her hands flew up to her breasts as she writhed. She squeezed and fondled them, bending her knees and spreading her legs wide so Arnie could center himself between them. He watched her and massaged her clit. And all the while the smudgy, ever-present images of the Others torqued her mind and mixed her desire for Arnie with her exhibitionist fantasies into a high-combustion time bomb.

She convulsed and begged for mercy. The atomic energy of explosive orgasm built to a frantic, shuddering crescendo, and right when she couldn't stand another second of his carnal torture, Arnie hoisted her hips and drove his cock into her.

A resonant cry shot up from her gut and barreled to the edges of the universe. It rolled over the rim like the steam off dry ice and bubbled down into the center of time.

Out there in the nothing, in the bright white spotlight, her soul ruptured in collision with his.

The impact froze them solid.

She had no idea how long they lay motionlessly fused. The radiant glow of his eyes began hypnotizing her and bathing her in a warm silver beam that played text on the screen of her mind like an old-fashioned movie projector.

*You belong to me.*

She cradled his face in her hands and broke the moment. Arnie's jaw clenched, his eyes closed, and he turned his face into her palm, kissing it with a possession so ferocious it seized his breath, and hers.

*Mine.*

And then he started moving inside her. Slowly, watchfully, mindful of her every response, he played with the mechanics of her body like the master engineer he was.

The ridges of his heavenly cock stroked her cunt like a textured condom. Only she hadn't required him to wear one. Unsafe sex at its finest, she thought briefly, and realized sex could never be safe with him.

He unhinged every section of her carefully soldered soul. She couldn't believe how *right* he felt. Dipping, lunging, circling.

The brush of his feverish skin against hers, melding their bodies into one singular sensation.

He filled her totally, grubbing deeply to grasp her heart and mind with a passion so intense and filling, it leaked out of her in tears.

*Mine. Mine. Mine.*

His slick, probing tongue on her flesh, suckling lips, gentle nibbles. Balls of lightning rolled through her body as his need for her peaked and he grew more demanding.

*Ava. Fuck me 'til I can't walk.*

She coiled her legs around his thrusting hips, urging his cock in deeper with her heels. Their stomachs slid together, apart, together. Her pebbled nipples nudged his satiny skin with each lunge and telegraphed dynamic messages to her clit.

He dipped his head down to nip her tender nipples and braced himself against the mattress with his hands. With a shudder, she slipped her hands underneath his, braiding fingers while his tempo against her G-spot increased.

*Faster*, she told him in her mind. *Fuck me like there's no tomorrow.*

His back arched and his hips pumped like pistons, shoving her down into the soft mattress. Clasping her fingers he lifted up enough for her to see his eyes, now darkened and heavy with mounting passion.

"God, Ava," he gasped, licking into her mouth. *You're what I want.*

"You are," she answered on a sigh.

She sucked on his tongue, tightening her lips around it then releasing and catching his raspy chin in her teeth. He playfully shook off and ground open lips over hers, consuming her mouth, her cheeks and roaming over her face in unbridled exploration.

*Could you love me?* His eyes bored into her, their energy making a complete loop inside her body. Caught in his net, she whimpered in surrender as harder and faster he pounded, until her tensing muscles cried out for release, finally detonating in a blast of fury.

*Yes!* She clenched him tighter as she screamed.

He cried out too, a guttural shout of triumph as he came, circling and plunging inside her. *Was that a yes to me, or to my cock?*

And finally, he sank on top of her in a puddle of spent fuel.

"So I guess you're not disgusted by me anymore," Ava said after a while.

He let go a weak rumble of laughter, rising up a notch to gaze tenderly into her face. Blowing a strand of hair off her forehead, he said, "I was never disgusted with you. Chrysler. You had me by the nozzle from the start."

She giggled. "Okay, by my profession, then."

He rolled over swiftly so as not to lose her, yanking her on top of his hard body with a satisfied sigh. "I suggest I'll get over it." He stroked her back in long, lazy circles. "I'm sorry about your dad."

"Hmm." She rested her cheek on his chest, petting his pecs and wiggling her hips lower to keep his thick, softening cock inside.

"That feels good," he drawled. "Do it again."

"This?" she patted his chest, "or this?" She contracted her pussy and gave his shaft a hard squeeze.

He shuddered in aftershocks of ecstasy. "The second one."

"Plenty more where that came from." For some reason, he stiffened. His eyes closed and his hands came up to scrape across his face. "Arnie, what's wrong?"

* * * * *

*Outside the assembly building, Ground Control powwows, unsure of the majestic Saturn Five's usefulness beyond the next few missions.*

She'd warned him she only wanted him temporarily. This was a fling for her, a vacation flirtation with the useless nerd.

Geek for a week.

He'd have laughed if it'd been funny.

He'd planned on steering clear for that reason, to guard his raw feelings. But her convictions, her mind and that freaky white hair had dismantled him and all his intentions.

If he'd kept out of her head he'd have been fine.

But the infinite reaches inside it, the sensation he got when he was in there of traveling back in time to the wondrous beginnings of the universe, changed everything.

He was jettisoning into unknown territory, new life, new civilizations. Tumbling through exploding nebulae.

Or maybe he was going quietly insane.

There wasn't one molecule of him she didn't own. He simply didn't belong to himself anymore. That only left one option—enjoy every last millimeter of her while she stuck around and stalk her to the ends of the galaxy when she left.

A primitive possessiveness spurted up from his core, firing the rocket boosters, instantly calcifying his dick and heaving him off his back. In one seamless motion he lifted her up and flipped her back to front so she was sitting on his legs. Reaching around her he grabbed both her tiny wrists in one hand, snatched the venetian blind cords from the casement that acted as a headboard, and lashed them together.

"I've never been tied to window treatments before," she tittered.

"Then you haven't lived." He scooted backwards on the mattress and pulled her along with him and as he did, the thin cords tautened and began raising the blinds like a curtain on a Broadway stage. "Showtime."

"You can't be serious!" she shrieked, but fumes of carnal excitement billowed out of her pores, intoxicating him and undamming his testosterone in a great, gushing flood. In the enormous nighttime blackness of the picture window, twin images appeared as sharply as a mirror. Their eyes met inside.

"I'm going to fuck you in front of the whole world," he declared.

"There's nothing out there but empty space," she protested. Then he saw her head turn.

Focusing on her actual profile he noticed her gaze shoot around the room and widen. He glanced around too before looking back at her. *You see them?*

*No. But they're here.*

*They know where you live. Where to find you.*

She nodded slightly and swallowed.

He wrapped his arms around her waist, hoisted her onto all fours and helped her steady herself on her tied hands. *There's no escape.*

"I know."

*They'll never leave you alone. And neither will I.* Rearing up on his knees he braced her ass in his hands and lowered his head to bite the tender white flesh of her cheeks.

She revolved her hips and moaned. "I don't want you to."

Her firm, peachy roundness tasted of sin between his teeth and he bore down harder than he'd intended. She yelped and squirmed and he had an evil urge to brand her with a hickey. *You can never prove we had this conversation.* Echoes of laughter laced with the scrap of a nervous giggle barged into in his mind.

God she was cute.

Time to take ownership. Put part of her inside him to act as a homing device if they got separated. He bit her again with the vague idea of eating a piece of ass. Her tailbone bucked against his nose as she shouted a protest and he almost stopped, but even as he bent his head to kiss it and make it better, she began to coo and groan in pleasurable echo.

"I never knew pain could feel so…so…"

"Good?"

"Yes," she sighed. "Bite me again. Harder."

"No." But he wanted to. Not to hurt her but to gnaw his way into her soul.

"Please." Her request rode out on a quaver that vibrated against his eardrums and tickled the pleasure sensors in his brain. He had her at his mercy. She was begging. Had any woman ever begged him for anything before? Not that he recalled. Damn, it felt good, and made him hornier than a geek had the right to be.

It was fun, too.

"Nah," he repeated, trying not to let the smile seep into his voice. "What if I draw blood?"

"Then drink it."

Fuck the torture. He needed that succulent mass between his teeth.

He grabbed fistfuls of flesh and pinched, his incisors chattering along the pinking crests, lips sucking and pulling until the pink splotches merged into a Red Spot of Jupiter on her butt.

She moaned and thrashed her head, lashing him repeatedly with her hair until his skin became so sensitized it felt like a face full of buckshot each time. Hurt so good. Now he knew what the hell that meant.

*Ava will hurt you so good.*

He closed his eyes tightly against a swift wave of panic. If she left him, he'd die. But she wouldn't. She couldn't. Because he wasn't going to let her. Instead he'd become her master, keep her begging, keep her wanting and keep her getting.

Straightening his spine with an injection of resolve, he opened her up and impaled her from behind.

She pitched and yawed—the molten heat exchange between her cunt and his dick nearly sending him into thermonuclear meltdown.

He plunged onward, pumping hard into her pussy, his tingling balls slapping her moist labia with every thrust. She slumped down on her elbows bringing her ass higher in the air and he leaned over her back and slid his hands around her rib cage.

In the window he watched himself driving into her. She lunged forward and back with each thrust, her pale hair a wild mop around her face. Through the silken strands he caught the green glitter of her eyes as she watched him fuck her too.

Then she began grinding her hips, using her knees to push backwards and smack his abdomen with her ass. She tossed her head and bit that luscious lower lip.

Hot semen dispersed through his pipes and he felt it rising through his shaft, a keening orgasm only a heartbeat away.

As if sensing his proximity to oblivion, her lips curled into a wicked grin and he stared in fascination, distracted for a split second. She met his gaze boldly, lifted her chin and clamped her legs together with a growl.

A great, shuddering roar ripped out of his lungs as she imprisoned his cock. Blistering bliss turned every nerve red-hot as steaming cum spurted out of his cock, deep into her. And with gigantic convulsions, he punched through the atmosphere in a cacophony that would've shattered a meteor. Jolting quakes rocked the bed, shimmying it several inches off center and sending him hurtling into an ecstasy he found only with her.

*Houston, I have no problems.*

Free from Earth's gravity, he floated joyously above her slender curves.

She kept her pussy cinched around his cock, binding him inside and swaying gently while the last dregs of cum dribbled out. Jagged arcs of static electricity crackled across his flesh, glowed blue for a second then dissolved in the air.

The old Arnie would've been freaked. The new Arnie wasn't surprised in the least. He expected the unexpected, now.

Overhead lay the cold vacuum of the unknown, below crouched the luminous woman he loved. He pressed his cheek into her shoulder giving thanks to the ancient primordial soup that spawned the life that became her.

And to think he'd thought she was from Pluto.

He chuckled tiredly, drawing her exhausted attention.

*What's funny?*

"Nothing." He flicked his tongue across her delicious nape. "Not a thing," he repeated before nuzzling as snugly as he could into her neck.

"Why'd you laugh?"

Her voice carried a sound of caution and hurt Arnie'd never heard. Most of his previous relationships had been long term but a real yawn, fizzling out in a see-ya-later type way. He'd never hurt a woman before.

Carefully, he rolled onto his side and pulled her down next to him. One long leg slithered over his and she angled her hips for full body contact. How had he lived so long without the kiss of her skin? "When I first met you, I had this loopy idea you were an alien. I was just remembering that."

She raised herself on one arm and grinned. "What a coincidence. I had the same thought about you."

Every cell in his body shriveled. "No shit." Yet another similarity. There was no doubt they had about a billion things in common. But as amazing as that seemed on the surface, it wasn't all that unusual. He had a theory that life was a giant vortex and people of the same density spilled out in the same place.

What bothered him about Ava were the specifics involved. Like her sensing the Observers. And, now, her thinking he was an alien.

Women had thought him strange before, but as far as he knew no one had ever questioned his planet of origin. Why now? *Why her?*

"You're very different from your siblings." *And from everyone else on Earth.*

Okay. The mind reading game was wearing thin. And freaking him out. Surely the thoughts he imagined as coming from her were really his own. Right? That's what happened when there was no blood in your brain. *Right?* "Yeah, I know. Nature fucks up once in a while."

In the end it was the only explanation for his presence amongst the Simpsons. Along the course of his life the sense of not belonging had followed him doggedly, feeding his insecurities and his anger. He'd tried on every single theory to figure out what had gone akimbo but none of them quite seemed to fit. Yeah. Nature fucked up once in a while. Weren't platypuses proof enough?

"True," she said playfully.

"You didn't have to agree," he snorted.

"Well, anyway." She bussed him on the nose. "You still think I'm an alien?"

"No. Now I *know* you are…" He looked up at her, returning the kiss on the tip of her all-too-human nose. "Because what just happened between us was out of this world." *Nice.* He patted himself on the back.

She cooed softy and melted in his arms. "It's never been this way for me. You're an incredible lover."

His chest swelled and he almost squeezed her in half out of gratitude. "You inspire me to greater heights."

"On the height scale, that was like…oh, let's see…the moon. What're you going to do for an encore?"

He leered at her. "Really want to know?"

Ava's eyes widened and a watery girlish giggle bubbled out of her throat. The pure femininity of that sound uncaged wild animal lust again and he vaulted over her, dragging her legs off the bed and hooking them over his shoulders.

"Oh my God!" she shrieked. "Not again. I can't take it!"

He smiled evilly into shocked eyes for two seconds before spreading her cunt and burying his mouth in it like a lion at the kill.

He hadn't remembered to untie her. But more importantly, she hadn't asked him to. As her chest rose and fell he caught glimpses of her arms stretched over her head, how helpless she was, how he had her under his command.

And fuck if she didn't love it. Perhaps she was one of those tightly controlled professional women who secretly yearned for sexual submission. He'd have to take note of this side of her so he could use it. Not against her, but for her. For him. For them both and their future.

Hours later, he puttered in the kitchen, cocky and blindingly happy. He constructed two monstrous deli sandwiches, grabbed two cold beers and bounded up the stairs back to Ava.

She snored gently in slumber, making tiny poofing noises. He got hard again thinking about those lips poofing around Saturn Five, as they'd done the night before. Setting the sandwiches on the table beside her, he crawled into bed and gently touched the cold bottle to one nipple.

Amazing how quickly the reaction came. She arched in sleep like a cat, hips doing automatic three-sixties. He pressed the bottle down again. This time, she moaned, hands heading south as the message was received.

Laughing soundlessly, he shackled both wrists in one hand, put the beer aside and took over where she left off. Incredible how fast those legs opened without her being aware of what was happening. He wondered if he could invade her dreams this way, make her think of him night and day.

Pressing her clit firmly with his thumb, he dipped a finger in her well and started tickling.

She bolted upright, hair flying. He shoved her back down and continued his mission, lustily enjoying her desperate undulations and the contraction and expansion of her slick, hot velvety interior against the flesh on his finger.

"You're a sadist," she gasped.

"Poor Ava," he sniggered. He hooked his finger inside her succulent cunt and rotated it gently, grazing and cupping her pubic bone and feeling her reactive spasm. Twitching his thumb against her nub, he bent his head to lap and suckle her labia, guaranteeing every inch of her pussy was lavished with attention.

"A beast, a devil, a…ah…ahhh…ahhhhhhh."

"Choo," Arnie supplied as she came. Phew, good thing he lived out here in the boonies. Those howls would've awakened the dead. He withdrew his finger and sucked her flavor off it like the salt on a pretzel stick.

"I'm glad you like how I taste," she said.

"Makes for a savory appetizer." He grinned. Bloated with a mischievousness he hadn't experienced since his teens, he set the sandwich on her heaving chest and sat back to eat. "Snack time," he said when she raised her head to peer at him.

"Oh goody," she muttered. "As if I could eat right now."

"You need your strength."

Sluggishly, she scooted back against a pile of pillows to sit up beside him. "You're telling me."

They dug in together, laughing, snorting beer and generally behaving like a couple of incorrigible kids.

Arnie never expected love to be this much fun. It blew him away to think of what he'd been missing while drowning in motor oil all day and carousing with pilots at night. No wonder he never saw Gage anymore.

All of a sudden, aeronautics had lost its luster, its ability to hold his attention and make him thirst for more knowledge, even if he never applied it.

The Entity changed everything. Now, he wanted to know *her* inside out. Wanted to spend the second part of his life learning every miniscule detail of that finely crafted body, that infinite mind.

If only she would let him.

Gazing dreamily at her, he realized he couldn't force anything on her. She was an independent woman who knew her own mind. But, that didn't mean he couldn't *persuade* her.

Tonight had been a good start. He'd received some crucial information and would have to stay alert for more, so he could plot the necessary adjustments to his mission objectives. With meticulous observation and a little luck, if she veered off course back toward Minneapolis, he'd be able to fire her engine for a free-return trajectory.

# CHAPTER SEVEN

The ringing phone slapped Ava out of a dream. She automatically lunged for it, drowsily assuming she was on call. "Dr. Ward."

She jerked the receiver away from her ear when she got blasted by an excited shriek. "Omigod, I knew you'd be there. It's Lorna."

Ava rubbed sleep out of her eyes and glanced over at Arnie stirring, arm slung over his face. She reached out to pet him awake. "I'm here all right," she said, stroking his silky warm shoulder. "You home yet?"

"Still in Madison. We're heading to the airport right now."

Ava glanced out the window to see the sun peeking over distant hills. Arnie rolled onto his side and tucked her close, nuzzling her sleepily.

"When I get back, you have to tell me everything," Lorna demanded. "But for now, did you?"

Fully aroused, Arnie nibbled along her neck, sliding a hand up to gently knead her breast. She felt one strong leg intertwine hers, his fuzzy hair tickling her thigh.

"I better go."

"Don't you dare!"

She softly replaced the phone in its cradle as Arnie flipped over and pulled her on top of him. By the time it started shrilling again, she was bouncing too high on his cock to answer.

Thirty minutes later they lounged in the bathtub and Ava had resumed shivering, but for entirely different reasons. For one thing, she could barely stand up after last night's activities. For another, she was overcome with emotion for this man.

He lay underneath—her own personal vibrating recliner—soaping her body in long swirling strokes and massaging the tense muscles in her back. She closed her eyes and leaned against his hot, wet chest. His hands came up under her arms to slip and slide across her abdomen. For a minute, she feared he'd move lower, but he stopped short and returned to her breasts.

Man, she needed a break. Not a long one. Just a chance to breathe and sort out her feelings.

There was no doubt in her mind she loved him. Desperately. On top of his myriad other fine qualities, he was the most sensitive lover she'd ever known. He watched her constantly, intently, reading her moods and desires with uncanny exactitude.

*Reading her mind.*

She shook her head. Couldn't be.

Last night, in the throes of animal passion she'd sworn they'd spoken to each other in thought waves. Had entire conversations, in fact. Now, in the satiated light of morning it seemed silly. A product of a love-starved, lust-drugged imagination.

At the most it'd been finely tuned intuition. After all, they were totally into each other and she'd heard that could happen with lovers.

And what a wild one he turned out to be. Her pulse sprinted at the memory. He could go from nerd-tinged rocket scientist to snorting sex beast in a heartbeat. She'd never met anyone like him.

And the best part was that he was her own scrumptious secret. She'd bet her 401k no one in town knew Arnie Simpson's capabilities, not even his ex-girlfriends. Ava instinctively knew he'd never behaved this way with anybody else. Neither had she.

Impulsively, she twisted around and grabbed his face for a smooch. They'd been figurative virgins yesterday. Today they were discovering the wonders of passion together.

"What was that for?" Arnie asked, laughing and swiping soap from his mouth.

"Because I love…"

Arnie stiffened, making her choke back her words, "Because I loved last night," she amended.

He relaxed and she breathed a sigh of relief. Obviously, love didn't fit into his equation. Well, what did she expect after the speech she gave him by the tree? Now he saw her as a good-time girl and had decided to take advantage. She deserved it. Damn.

She hadn't reckoned on falling head over heels. To think she'd considered him fling material. She could kick herself, knowing how inventive, how philosophical, how much darn fun he turned out to be.

Suddenly, the rest of her life yawned before her and she didn't want the second half to be like the first—full of books and ambition. She wanted Arnie—his laugh, his dumb jokes, his stream-of-consciousness monologues and satiny muscled flesh. How could she face life without him, having seen how perfectly they fit?

She wished she could rewind the tape and edit in new dialogue. If she could, she'd tell him she wasn't the type for a fling either, but the distance between them frightened her. His inability to support a family frightened her. Small towns frightened her.

Ava was a big thinker. So was Arnie. How could either of them be confined in a place like Flintlock? The damn universe wasn't large enough to corral his mind. How could he tolerate living here?

While they toweled off and got dressed, Ava devised a master plan. She had to find out what internal obstacles kept him from a lofty profession, what kept him here. That way, maybe, she'd be able to convince him grow. And to leave.

"What time do you have to go to Lorna's?" Arnie asked over breakfast. "Gage is bringing his stuff here after lunch."

Lord, she'd practically forgotten the wedding. Lorna might have last-minute details to attend. Glancing at the clock, Ava realized they must be home by now, having called her at dawn. Dread flooded through her, time with Arnie winding down.

Lorna and Gage were staying in a friend's lakeside cabin tonight and the next night, leaving her one full day to recover from the party before heading back to work. Then they'd fly her to Minneapolis on their way to a Canadian honeymoon.

"I guess I should go soon," she said, too sad to meet his eyes.

He reached over, grabbed her chin and tilted her face his way. "Stay with me tonight."

She looked at him, surprising a worried gleam in his eyes. "Of course." As if he could keep her away. "Can I sleep here tomorrow night too?"

"I suggest you can sleep here forever if you want." He rose to clear the dishes.

He spoke the words as if they were no big deal. But her antennae went up. She studied his back while he puttered. Powerful emotions rolled off him like nitrogen gas, swirling around her, taking a ride on her breath, down her throat and into her gut. Her heart seized in epiphany. Had she really been that stupid? She flashbacked to all that had happened yesterday, the clues he had dropped at her feet.

He loved her.

She needed no further evidence.

Rising, she went up behind him, wrapping her arms around his sinuous waist and pressing her breasts into his back. He groaned and leaned into her embrace. She held him that way for a moment before sliding round in front, between him and the sink.

His head was bowed chin to chest, his breathing uneven. Ava kissed the top of his head.

"Arnie," she sighed. "Look at me."

When he lifted his face, the tortured emotions etched on his features nearly sent her to her knees. Closing her eyes tightly against the tidal wave of passion, she brushed the tip of her nose around his cheeks, his nose, his mouth. She latched on to his lips with her own, seeking the solace and safety only he could provide. "I want to sleep with you forever," she breathed against them. "Arnie, I—"

The phone rang, its old-fashioned bell reverberating through the house and making her jump. She slumped against Arnie, feeling his arms tighten in reassurance.

"That would be Lorna," he said.

She nodded tiredly. "We'll talk later."

"I suggest you better not forget what you were going to tell me." With understanding chuck under her chin, Arnie picked up the phone and handed it directly to her.

"Help!" Lorna yelped.

"I'm on my way," she said.

* * * * *

Arnie dropped her off, singed her with his signature kiss then headed over to his folks to see if he could help with the hog roast.

Ava stumbled up the three stairs to Lorna's front door, barely able to lift her legs. Before going in, she paused to pinch the bridge of her nose against a developing headache.

How she would make it through the day with all the movement a wedding required was beyond her. If last night was a taste of what she was in for loving Arnie, she could happily cancel her gym membership and sock all that money away for sex toys.

Grinning at the thought, she let herself in the front door and was met with Judith Merryfield's patrician scowl. "I can't believe any daughter of mine would choose calla lilies for a wedding."

Apparently, Judith was in Gage's court on that one.

Off in a corner, Lorna slumped in a chair, one leg over the arm, polishing her toenails. "It's a private joke, Mother. Something between me and Gage."

"But this is a public ceremony. What will everyone think?"

"I really don't care." Lorna shrugged.

Judith threw up her hands and turned to Ava. "See what's happened to her since she moved here? I need strong tea." She exited stage left.

Ava tossed Lorna a sneaky smile, crossing the room and removing the nail polish from her hand. "Let me do that."

Lorna leaned back with a sigh. "She's been carping about my choices all morning. About the only thing she likes in this whole mess is Gage. At least he won her heart."

"How could he not?"

"Speaking of winning hearts, how did last night go, alone with Arnie?"

Ava felt the heat course up her cheeks as her grin spread ear to ear. No use trying to hide anything. She didn't really want to anyway. "He's amazing," she sighed.

Lorna leaned forward and tipped up her chin. She gazed long and hard into Ava's eyes before sitting back with a satisfied smirk. "You look just like I do after Gage finishes with me."

"I suggest those two went to the same school," Ava quipped, dissolving into giggles.

"Birds of a feather," Lorna said. "Still, I'm surprised. He's so…restrained."

"No he's not." Ava switched feet.

"Not what?" Gage asked, coming into the living room.

Ava glanced up and flipped her hair over a shoulder. "Nothing."

Gage measured their faces and narrowed his eyes. "Is there something I should know?

"I suggest you go ask your friend," Lorna snickered.

Gage's eyebrows shot up as he flicked a glance at Ava. She gave him a sweet smile and raised her eyebrows right back.

Gage grew still for a minute while he processed the information, then a wolfishly evil grin spread across his handsome face. "I might have to go see Arnie earlier than I'd planned."

"We'll be wanting a full report," Lorna said.

Ava shook her head. "No we won't. No post-mortems this time." She felt protective of their privacy and hoped Lorna wouldn't press for details. They'd always shared everything until Gage came along. She hoped Lorna would remember how that had felt.

Lorna and Gage stared at her thoughtfully then exchanged a meaningful glance. He cleared his throat. "I doubt Arnie would tell me anything anyway. Never has before."

After Gage left, Lorna said. "I knew you'd fall in love with him. He's such a decent guy. I bet he loves you too."

"We didn't get the chance to talk about it," Ava hedged. She didn't want Lorna to feel badly about interrupting them—this was her wedding, after all! "But I think he feels the same way. I just have to figure out the logistics."

"Shouldn't be a problem."

Easy for Lorna to say. She'd been more than thrilled to chuck everything and immerse herself in Flintlock society—if it could be called that. Of course, her job could be done via wire services. Ava didn't have that kind of leeway. But, unwilling to get gloomy yet, she attacked Lorna's toes with renewed vigor then reached for her hand. "I'm going to convince him to move to Minneapolis. There have to be at least a dozen engineering companies."

"I can't imagine Arnie in a suit, in an office."

"That's where he belongs. His talent is wasted out here."

"But he's happy," Lorna said quietly. Her expression made Ava's spine ripple.

"He'd be happier utilizing his brain. Trust me."

"Airplane maintenance is nothing to sneeze at, Ava. A lot of pilots depend on Arnie. He's got a national reputation for excellence."

Ava sat back on her heels, blowing a strand of hair off her forehead and trying not to sound as ticked off as she felt. "Whose side are you on, anyway?"

Lorna's brow furrowed, concern entering her eyes. "Didn't know I had to choose."

Before Ava could answer Edward Merryfield lunged into the room, followed closely by his wife.

"Give me a hug." He swooped down, scooped her off the floor and into a warm embrace.

Judith rolled her eyes. "Ever since he spent a long weekend here at the annual pork-n-brew festival, he hasn't been the same."

"Betty the florist changed his life by doing the Macarena with him," Lorna supplied. "Don't listen to Mother. Secretly, she likes his new loosey-goosey image."

"No, I don't," Judith said. But a gleam in her eye belied her words. "Speaking of flowers, I'm going to trot over to the church to help Betty arrange the bouquets. Edward, why don't you take Gage to pick up the tuxedos? Who's that young man acting as best man?"

"Arnie Simpson," Lorna said.

"From the hog farm?" Judith scowled.

"From the airport," Ava replied. "He's an aeronautical engineer. Went to MIT on full scholarship."

Judith appraised her, eyes and nostrils flaring coyly. "I see," she murmured. "What's he doing out here, then?"

"That's what we'd all like to know," Ava said.

"Interesting," Edward put in. "I'll have to collar him for a chat. I know a company that's looking for a bright, young star."

A small glimmer of hope flashed in her heart and Ava coiled her arm through his. "Why don't you do that?" She smiled. "I'd like him to move a little closer to me."

Edward gazed down at her fondly. Because she was a doctor, like him, he'd assumed the role of mentor when she and Lorna met. Over the years, he'd become a surrogate father as well. "Whatever my second daughter wants," he intoned, patting her hand.

"Chop-chop." Judith clapped. "Time's a-wasting."

Everyone scattered to their various chores, leaving Lorna and Ava alone in the small house and in charge of last-minute cosmetic emergencies. They meandered into the bathroom to examine the colors Judith had selected.

"I'd be careful when approaching Arnie," Lorna said, revisiting the topic. "He's stayed put all these years for a reason."

"Maybe he didn't have a good enough reason to leave," Ava argued. "NASA isn't for everyone, you know. Maybe he hasn't explored other opportunities." It was a lame statement but she stuck with it for argument's sake. Lorna's comments caused a heavy feeling in her gut she didn't want to examine too closely right now.

"NASA isn't the only company chasing him. It's just the most high profile. That's why everyone talks about it."

Ava threw out her arms. "What am I going to do, sell my half of the practice and move to Flintlock?"

"It ain't so bad."

"I'd lose my edge out here in the country. Get lazy. People's health might be at risk. My father's doctors didn't make him see a specialist until it was too late. They'd gotten complacent."

"Oh honey. That's awful. I didn't know. But are you sure? I mean, you're talking malpractice here."

"My mother settled with them."

"Ava, why didn't you ever tell me?"

"I never told anyone. Doesn't look good when doctors sue other doctors. I wasn't one then, but, well, I guess I'm ashamed. I mean, all doctors make mistakes. And these guys were contrite. They didn't try to cover it up or make excuses like most doctors would. But still, my dad died because of negligence. Negligence that came from years upon years of practicing humdrum, everyday medicine. I couldn't live with myself if I became like that, and the wide variety of patients I see in the city keeps me on my toes."

"Well," Lorna said slowly. "You know better than I do." She sighed, taking Ava into her arms for a hug. "Don't worry. It'll work out."

"What if it doesn't?" Ava asked miserably.

"It will. Look at me and Gage. Here I was, caught up in the rat race, denying my true self and what I wanted and needed when he came along. He's restored my faith in the power of true love. What if Gage had given up, not pursued me like he did?" Lorna shuddered at the thought. "But he never gave up. You shouldn't either. Don't try to change Arnie, though. It'll backfire right in your sweet face."

"I don't really want to change him," Ava said softly. "I just want to be with him. I can't do that here."

"Well," Lorna sighed. "Maybe you won't have to. Maybe you're right and he'd be happier doing something else. I can't see it though."

"It's not like he's close with his family—"

"Wrong. They might bore him senseless and he might complain but he spends a lot of time with them. He really enjoys his nieces and nephews. Dotes on them. I'm surprised he hasn't mentioned it."

When had they bothered to discuss family? They'd been too busy ripping off each other's clothes. She hadn't wasted a speck of time thinking about the personal bonds that might shackle him to Flintlock. It gave her pause. Was she that absorbed in her work, that removed from a sense of family and community? Obviously, she was.

Ava couldn't recall the last time she'd called her mother in Fairbanks or spent an hour catching up with her brother in Germany. Her family was so far-flung across the globe she barely spared them a thought anymore.

How depressing.

All these years she'd been frantically keeping death at bay, keeping other families together while ignoring her own.

"Where are you going?" Lorna asked as Ava dove out the bathroom door.

"To call my mom," she said in a watery voice.

* * * * *

At last it was time to get dolled up. Judith fussed and clucked like a mother hen as she fastened Lorna into her corset, billowed the crinoline over her head, down her waist and pulled the strings tightly, like Mammy did for Scarlett.

Lorna's gown was strapless and tight along the bodice, nothing but netting from her waist to the floor. She resembled a Degas ballerina, a fluffy concoction made for tasting.

Ava squeezed into her shell-pink watered-silk sheath, lifting her arms when Judith flitted over to zip her up. The woman was a dynamo as well as a perfectionist. As annoying as she could be, both Ava and Lorna were thankful for her controlling nature today. She made sure their faces were exquisitely made up—not one mascara clump to be found. Their lips glistened enticingly, skin flawlessly smooth and eyes dark and smoky from the carefully blended eye shadow.

If she'd used a heavy hand with the cosmetics, she made no apologies. Photographers' lights washed you out. More makeup was a necessity. Tomorrow, those pictures would be all you had left.

She knew.

Both the women's hair had been artfully swept off their necks in French twists. The severity of her styling kept every hair in place, no tendrils allowed! Tonight, the eyes were the main focus. Not hair, not jewelry, not even dresses.

When she finally slipped Lorna's floor-length veil in place, anchoring it with a mouthful of bobby pins, all three women stepped back from the mirror and stared.

"Oh, Lorna," Ava choked. Even Judith welled up at the sight.

"I can't believe it's me," Lorna whispered. "Mother, you're a master."

"That's mistress, darling," Judith corrected, but her voice wobbled too much to sound harsh. "I've never seen a more luscious bride. Have you, Ava?"

Ava shook her head.

"Come on, darling. The photographer's in the living room and your father's waiting. Oh my. I can't wait for Edward to see you."

Ava went in first and stood across the room to get a better view of Edward's face when Lorna entered. She intended storing the memory of his emotional expression in her heart and bringing it out for her own wedding someday. Suddenly, she missed her father fiercely, knowing he would never give her away. But seeing Edward stunned speechless and trembling would just have to do.

He could barely control himself for the photo session, kept muttering about his little girl. Ava recorded every word, every glance and by the time they headed out to Gage's black London cab, was trembling herself.

The church sat perched by itself on the hem of town and Edward drove slowly. When they turned onto the street, he said, "I'll idle here a few minutes until everyone has gone inside. Wouldn't want to spoil your grand entrance."

Two of Arnie's hulking brothers were standing sentry on the sidewalk. They spied the cab and signaled the all clear.

Getting Lorna neatly out of the cab proved somewhat difficult, but they managed and swept into the church lobby without ensnaring too much debris in the tulle.

Tiny Simpson came up behind Judith, taking her elbow.

"Allow me to escort you to your seat, ma'am."

Judith turned with a polite smile that turned into a yelp of fright when she saw the mountain that was Tiny. It made everyone laugh and suddenly the mood changed from heavy nostalgia to effervescent joy. Edward turned to Lorna, carefully pulled her veil over her face and enshrouded her in a mist of dewy netting.

"I love you, Daddy."

The organ music swelled, the doors flung open and Ava turned down the aisle. Arnie stood at the other end.

His silvered gaze pinned her in its spotlight and she advanced, feeling like a singer coming out on stage. The closer she got, the brighter the light grew. He didn't smile, not once, but he did lick his chops before straightening his shoulders and clasping his hands over his crotch. He looked devastating in suit and tails, hair gelled back neatly off his face.

And, oh yeah, Gage looked nice too.

Ava remembered him just in time to savor his first glimpse of Lorna as she entered the nave.

He swayed from the impact. Arnie placed a discreet hand on his back to brace him. Gage grinned, a huge, dazzling smile that lit up the church like a sunrise. Arnie grinned along with him, watching Lorna, his lips moving as he spoke low words to his best friend.

What a moment for these two men, Ava thought. Two brothers about to welcome a woman between them. She wondered how Arnie felt about it. If he grieved as she had when she'd first felt Lorna's emotional absence. She'd have to ask him later.

Lorna arrived beside her, handed Ava her calla lilies and turned to face her father. He gently lifted the veil off her face, pressed a lingering kiss on her cheek, then took her hand and placed it in Gage's before sitting down next to Judith.

"Dearly beloved, we are gathered here today…"

Ava tried to pay careful attention during the ceremony. Lorna was unlikely to recall any of it and Ava wanted to notice the funny little mishaps that invariably occurred. From time to time, she snuck a glance at Arnie, but he seemed absorbed in the minister's words.

Finally, the big moment arrived.

"Do you, Gage Archer, take this woman—"

"I do."

"Let me finish," the minister joked.

Everyone in the church cracked up.

Arnie's gaze locked on Ava's, true and unwavering and astoundingly sincere. When Lorna said "I do", Ava's lips mouthed the words.

Arnie blinked and gave his head a vigorous shake. The recessional music blared. Gage and Lorna kissed. The entire town stood and cheered as they fled down the aisle. Then Arnie put her hand over his arm and boldly kissed her before they started down too.

"You know," he grinned as they reached the receiving line, "it's not polite to upstage the bride."

"Can't be helped when a man like you is watching."

"Oh yeah? What kind of man do you suggest I am?"

She scooched closer, laced her fingers through his and gazed at him. "My man."

His hand pumped hers like a heartbeat and his eyes went from silver to pearly white. "Hold that thought."

Wedding guests mobbed the hallway.

# CHAPTER EIGHT

Out on the airport highway under a pink and navy canopy with Venus plotting the course, Arnie fired the boosters on the speedster.

The sleek little car pounced away from the church toward the empty horizon and Ava fell back against the seat. "This is fabulous!" The wind took her words away so she merely stared at him, willing his concentration on the road to falter.

On cue his hand left the gearshift and found her thigh. They flew through the darkening sky. Ava saw the yellow lights and circus tents of the reception approaching. Cars mauled the open field next to a sprawling ranch house and a string of red brake lights formed a comet tail along the entryway. Ava expected to slow down and turn in.

The speedster's engine never stuttered.

"Hey," she shouted.

Arnie didn't look at her but his head tilted and a wicked grin curled the side of his mouth. *Ever make love in a rocket ship?*

Adrenaline pushed through her veins and made her dizzy. Did he mean literally?

He didn't slow down. She cast a fearful look ahead and saw nothing but space. Did this road go all the way into Madison? Was there anything in between?

Stars began littering the sky, popping out one after another as the last thin ribbon of pink light drooped below the land. Half expecting a flying saucer to materialize and catch her in its beam, she glanced back at Arnie.

As family after family had moved down the receiving line, her love for him had swelled her heart to bursting. He'd interacted with the whole town, introducing her to everyone, keeping a possessive arm around her waist and fielding the interested glances of other men with a vibrant chatter of invisible code.

They'd all seemed to catch it. As if they had antennae set up to receive it.

As if he had an extra sense. Another way to communicate.

*Get on my lap, woman!*

Everyone had automatically welcomed her with open arms, even as they silently acknowledged Arnie's claim.

Maybe the mind waves she'd gotten from him last night *were* real.

Which also made the current ones real.

*Let's have a close encounter of the lurid kind.*

She searched the darkness for his face and found nothing but twin stars twinkling back at her. Stars that were not in the sky. *Mood eyes, my ass. He doesn't have ordinary moods. Doesn't have ordinary thoughts. Everyone here knows he's not normal.*

But, he was respected and valued by the community. And why not? He was one in a million—make that a quintillion. You'd have to be an idiot not to take advantage of his talents. And Flintlock didn't seem peopled with idiots.

Had they taken him in? Nurtured him as their own? Pretended he was one of them so he'd stay and make their lives easier?

A meteor streaked across the heavens and fizzled in some deep, velvet pocket of atmosphere. An acrid odor like burning hair hit her nostrils and she blew it back out.

Arnie flinched, looked up and sent his searchlights into high beam. Had he smelled it too?

She shrugged. Most likely a hog from the reception. Smell carried.

Wrinkling her nose, she reached up to free her hair from Judith's bobby-pin piñata. She really had to get a grip. She'd been working too hard and not playing enough. Was probably teetering on exhaustion and should be hospitalized. Why else would she assume the aliens had landed? And that Arnie was one of them?

His genius made him weird, that's all. It wasn't as if she'd never met a genius before. She was one, for crying out loud.

Arnie was no more an alien than she.

A gust of wind hit them broadside. Both her hair and the bobby pins flew out of her hands. With a shriek, she automatically turned to grab for them, cursed herself for an idiot and settled back into her seat. Like hairpins were worth risking life and limb for.

Arnie's warm fingertip nudged her shoulder. She looked at him and he held out a closed fist. Opening her palm underneath, her jaw unhinged as he dropped a thin metal object into her hand.

*No way. Now way. No way.*

It must've fallen into his lap.

No way did he pluck it out of the jet stream.

"Where did you get this?" she howled.

His eyelids fell to half-mast and he smiled. Casually, he leaned over and took it in his teeth, spinning it around in his mouth with his tongue.

Her pussy played bongo drums.

Hiking up her skirt, she tore her stockings off and tossed the shreds into the wind too. Arnie came on full alert and fumbled with his fly. At the same time he scooted the driver's seat backwards to make more room between him and the steering wheel.

She slid onto his lap, her back to him, and felt his engorged cock settle between her slick labia. Grabbing the steering wheel, she braced her feet on the floor and lifted her ass.

*Boing!*

His cock popped upright and its huge, swollen head poked into her cunt.

Then his hands went around his shaft, guiding it, twirling it against her for a moment. She sat down with a thump and he filled her.

While his hips thrust gently, he pulled her back against his chest. "Keep steering." His voice came on a whisper into her ear. "Keep us on the road."

She fell into a trance and stared ahead, the wind in her hair, his hands at her waist and his cock pumping slowly and steadily inside her.

He took something from his mouth. The hairpin.

A tender hand moved between her legs and she felt the slender metallic slide of the pin against her clit.

Like a little magic wand it stroked her. The narrowness of it teased her nerve endings and brought them into focus like nothing she'd ever experienced before.

"Concentrate," he coaxed.

So she did. On the sight of the road, the scent of the wind, the sounds of the engine and the roar of her blood. The touch of his pleasure instrument against her clit and his cock inside her cunt. All her bodily senses locked and loaded.

Then there were the other ones.

A cacophony of voices filled her head. A garbled tangle of communications like a roomful of party conversation. And there were images too. The same ones she always had of people, but more of them. A giant crowd circling her and Arnie. Watching. And what was that? Clapping?

*Let go! Let go!* the voices chanted. *Steer with your energy.*

This was crazy. Had she gone insane without noticing or was lust gobbling her mind so thoroughly she'd lost the ability to reason?

*Steer with your heart. It knows the way home.*

That's good, she thought. Because she certainly didn't know where it was anymore. Yesterday she'd thought it was Minneapolis. Today she knew it couldn't possibly be anywhere Arnie wasn't.

Everything she knew and everything she wanted was bending and curling into shapes she didn't recognize. The entire world, the known universe in fact, had shifted underfoot until she no longer felt assured. Even her mind, once so dependable, seemed to be slipping.

*Let go!* a lone baritone commanded.

The crowd parted and a giant, hazy being stepped forward. Physically perfect and imposing, handsome and formidable, he looked like an ancient warrior or a guardian angel.

*I am Anthros. I've monitored your mission. Now it is time to fulfill the objectives I've mapped for you and let go. His destiny depends upon it.*

Whose destiny?

*Michael's.*

Who the hell was Michael? A white light detonated in her brain, obscuring her sense of reason. Her eyeballs fluttered in their sockets and her vision fogged. The wind must've dried them out. She blinked rapidly several times, and by the time she could see and think clearly again, the crowd had disappeared into the fading light.

The only thing that remained in front of her now was a ribbon of road that started in a big city, and dead-ended in a one-horse town.

Her path no longer appeared familiar, yet she sensed underneath it still was, that she would indeed get what she wanted, but not quite in the way she'd envisioned. The key was to stop trying to manipulate everything to suit her own ends.

*Today's words of wisdom brought to you by Anthros, the imaginary gladiator.*

Who was that armored man? Her subconscious made flesh, or her guardian angel? His command seemed to bridge the fracture between indecision and action. Why shouldn't she take his advice? She'd heard far dumber recommendations in her life than his.

Sucking in a deep breath, she focused on the road ahead, released the steering wheel and spread her arms to the fates.

Arnie wielded his hairpin with the precision of a neurosurgeon. His other hand gripped her ass and pulled her firmly onto his lap. He held her there and circled his hips, no longer thrusting. Just circling. Until the fullness of him, the ridged texture of his cock, the keen focus of the hairpin, the wind, the speed, the universe's eyes upon her and the sheer danger of their predicament stimulated her to a shattering crescendo.

Then he gunned it.

The speedster screamed down the highway. Which was a good thing. Because her orgasmic screams would've aroused every village into Madison.

She squirmed on his cock while the powerful jolts rocked through her, arms out, head thrown back, eyes closed tightly, and as she heard him moaning in climax, she could've sworn the speedster went airborne.

* * * * *

"I get such strange thoughts whenever we make love," Ava said as they drove slowly back to the festivities.

"Good strange or bad strange?"

She turned her upper body toward him and leaned against the door. "Not sure. Just strange. Pure strange."

"Name one."

She ruminated a moment, trying to tease out a good example. "Well, there are always people watching."

He nodded.

"This time they spoke to me and told me that someone named Michael depended on me."

"Do you know anyone named Michael?"

"Not yet."

"I suggest you're not going to, either. Unless he's a toothless old man on his deathbed."

"Jealous much? But more importantly, they also told me to let go of the steering wheel and navigate with my heart."

He snorted. "Good thing you didn't listen."

She blinked. "But I did listen. I let go."

He tossed her an amused look. "No you didn't. I was watching to make sure your orgasm didn't get us both killed. Guess it was a pretty good one."

Better than she'd realized if it'd stolen her mind.

Hadn't she let go? She could've sworn she did. Yet he said she hadn't.

What was happening to her? Her heart started pounding. Insanity did *not* run in her family. No history of it whatsoever. "Arnie, I'm scared."

"Of what?"

"Of all the crazy ideas I'm getting. I'm coming unhinged."

He pulled the car over, killed the engine and wrapped her in his arms. "I suggest the sex is blowing our minds. I get freaky thoughts too, but then, I always get freaky thoughts. Sex with you just intensifies them. It's never been like this for me."

"Me either. But what do you think it means? Are these images real or am I hallucinating? I *hear* them speak to me. And I mentally obeyed a dangerous command. They told me to steer with my heart."

His grip on her arm tightened and his fingers kneaded the flesh on her upper arm while he thought. "Sounds like a metaphor," he muttered. "Maybe it's your subconscious telling you to follow your heart in your dealings with me."

"That's some vivid subconscious I've got, then."

"Just don't let yourself be hypnotized by it next time."

Easier said than done, it seemed. "And then there's this telepathic communication between us. Do you 'hear' my thoughts as if I've spoken them out loud? I hear yours."

He glanced at her and nodded. "I think I do. I'm getting close to being convinced they're for real."

"Arnie, we're not normal."

"Took you long enough."

She clenched her teeth. "Please stop teasing. We need to find out what's going on. What if—I'm not saying this is true—but what if one of us isn't quite human?"

"If one or both of us is super-human then it's probably some genetic, evolutionary leap. We're used to not noticing that shit because it happens so slowly. Perhaps with us, it speeded up. I suggest that's completely out of our control and there's no use worrying about it." He appeared relaxed but his free hand pumped the steering wheel, the skin on his knuckles turning alternately bone-white and tan.

"But aren't you curious? Don't you want to know why ghosts seem to be watching us and why we can communicate telepathically?"

"Not sure if knowing why would help anything."

"Some scientist you are!"

"I suggest I'm being philosophical. That's a science. Even if it is abstract and moronic sometimes."

She poked him in the ribs and he laughed. Then he said, "We can't change the facts about us or our relationship. Maybe it's better not to dig too deeply for answers."

Interesting. Was he being honest or was he distressed at venturing out of his comfort zone? "Are you scared what the answers might be?"

He pinned her with an intense gaze. "No. It's too big to be scared of. It's the little shit that scares the crap out of me." The focused light in his eyes softened. "Heck, I'd be thrilled if one of us turned out to be Superfreak. Wouldn't you?"

"Well, yes, but—"

"Then just go with it."

*That's what Anthros said.* "How?"

"Our story is just beginning. Don't skip to the middle or read the ending before we've even gotten started." He shrugged. "Take this one paragraph at a time or you'll flip out."

Like she hadn't already? Okay. Okay. "Oh Arnie. What are we going to do?"

He opened his mouth as if to say something and a bright glare of headlights illuminated his face. Ava squinted and held up a hand.

A faded red pickup pulled alongside and Tiny Simpson leaned out of the cab. "Hate to interrupt you two lovebirds," his voice boomed. "But Lorna and Gage are about to have their first dance and I got sent to find you."

"Be right there," Arnie said. Tiny's truck lurched forward, made a u-turn and roared back down the road.

Arnie turned to her and smiled regretfully. "We'll figure that out later. Right now, I suggest we're going to Disney World."

They finished the drive in contemplative silence and as they parked the car and approached the reception, the aromas of roasting pork, sugary cake icing and alcohol-laden drinks teased her nostrils. A swift, fierce hunger struck her gut and her mouth watered. Then another odor piggybacked in and slapped her head out of the storm clouds.

Hog farm.

Judging by the general merriment of the guests, she alone noticed it. But the nauseating scent sent her reeling and searching desperately for salvation.

What she saw made her stomach lurch.

Portable toilets.

Gag.

Now their odor swirled into the mix.

Appetite thoroughly ruined, she smiled wanly when she spied Lorna waving frantically from the bandstand. Feeling like a bad friend for being so easily distracted from Lorna's special day, and for being so consumed with her own troubles, she waggled her fingers with fake enthusiasm and stretched her lips over clenched teeth.

From across the room, Lorna froze and glowed. Ava's facial muscles relaxed and her smile became more genuine as achy yearning yielded to pure love. They grinned at each other while tears pricked her eyes then the band played "Unforgettable" and Gage swept Lorna out onto the plywood dance floor.

"I suggest that's a good tune," Arnie said quietly. She felt a featherlight hand at her nape.

"One of my favorites," she murmured, leaning into him and wrapping an arm around his lean waist.

"Never was one of mine." He appeared to be watching the newlyweds but his eye was on her. "Until now."

"No matter what happens, I'll never forget you."

"I think I was born remembering you."

A hiccough lodged in her throat. He had that knack for saying what lay in her heart. How could she go on without him? How did she survive before?

Under any other circumstances, this would be the moment they professed undying love, but she couldn't yet. She couldn't because this was Lorna's party, *and* they'd have to discuss living arrangements and his future employment.

Her throat constricted at the thought. Once the "I Love Yous" were spoken, the deal breakers had to be discussed and she wasn't ready to uncover and confirm those yet. Tonight, she wanted the fantasy. And the next night. And the night after that. She wanted to be totally and utterly impractical and she wanted to stay that way forever and never go back to real life.

For the first time, she truly wished he *was* an alien. An alien *commander*. From Planet Pleasure.

Maybe then he could abduct her and she'd simply be forced to live a different life. The decision would be out of her control.

The dance ended and everyone made a mad dash for the food. She and Arnie threaded their way to a table after a hefty platter of piggy was pushed into her hands.

She sighed.

She loved Arnie. This was the family he came with. And the pig was delicious. Truly. If only the smells would disappear she'd be fine. But they wouldn't.

As if the hog smells weren't enough, the Simpsons welled in and invaded their table and all the surrounding tables. Ray and Marty, the youngest brothers, took up residence next to Arnie.

"Isn't the band great?" gushed Myra, easing her bulbous stomach into the seat next door.

Ava breathed through her mouth and tried to smile. "Wonderful." And it was true. The jazzy swing music Lorna had chosen set a perfect, joyful tone that would've normally inspired Ava to get up and dance. Maybe later, if her stomach started cooperating.

"You won't believe this, but a few months ago, I was as slim as Lorna." Myra smiled. Her husband, Donny, hung an arm across her shoulders.

"She sure was," he confirmed. "Prettiest girl in town. And you're the second prettiest."

She blinked at the flood of warmth his simple statement brought. It was the kind of well-mannered compliment she'd previously only heard in movies—usually uttered by a man in a cowboy hat—and minus the smug smile she would've expected as punctuation.

Sincere or not, this man had been raised right. Myra'd caught herself a winner.

Nora joined the party. "Don't make me jealous with baby talk," she warned Myra with a grin. Then she explained to Ava, "I can't get knocked up to save my life. Been trying for months."

"What kind of underwear does your husband wear?" Ava asked automatically. Shocked silence blanketed the table. Arnie raised his eyebrows at her.

Nora squirmed and braided her fingers tightly. "Briefs," she said in a small voice. Her eyes tiptoed around the table, checking in with the others as if making sure she hadn't overstepped her bounds.

Everyone watched Ava closely and showered Arnie with sidewise glances.

"Too tight," Ava said in her most professional voice. "Tomorrow, I want you to run down to the Emporium and buy him some boxers. Here," she scribbled her phone number on a napkin. "Call me in two months."

Nora took the napkin and stared at it. "You're a doctor?"

"Yes," Ava nodded. "I'm a proctologist."

Everyone gasped. Arnie winced at her candor but she felt it best to just lay it on the line immediately. They were bound to find out anyway.

Tiny Simpson took a long, slow sip of coffee and stared at her. Even though his father sat nearby, it became clear that somewhere along the line, Tiny had assumed alpha position.

"So you're telling us briefs are no good if men want to make babies?"

Ava met his gaze squarely. "The constricting nature of briefs can make the temperature in the scrotum too high, killing sperm. Changing to boxers might not work, but it's worth a shot before paying gobs of money to a fertility clinic."

A murmur looped around the table. Consultations were held. Ultimately, Tiny turned to Nora. "Tell Charlie I said it was okay."

Nora let out a tense breath. Apparently, nothing got done in this family without Tiny's approval—even changing underwear.

Ava dropped her head into her hands. Arnie reached out and massaged her shoulders, throwing her an understanding glance when she peeked at him through her fingers.

Tiny leaned back, metal folding chair squealing under his weight. He tucked a thumb in his waistband, edging it around the circumference of a considerable stomach.

"We have to go all the way into Friend's Ferry for an examination," he said, sweeping a paw to include all the men. They nodded somberly. "Over a hundred miles."

Ava pressed her lips together and nodded back.

"That's a long way to go to have your ass examined."

A general laugh went up.

"Me?" he continued. "I prefer a woman doctor."

Ava felt her eyes widen. The whole table leaned forward. No one breathed.

He smiled slyly. "Smaller fingers."

"Oh my Lord!" The women whooped, scarlet faces bent low over the table. A massive giggle gurgled up through Ava's chest, and out in a guffaw that even startled Arnie.

She met Tiny's eyes and laughed harder, right along with him, and bonded with the down-home wisdom in his amused gaze. As an encore, she held up her hand for inspection, sending the pregnant Simpsons to the bathroom and the men to the ground.

When they'd recovered and returned, Tiny hoisted himself up, circled around and laid a hand on her shoulder. "You're all right," he said, before ambling off for more hog.

Immediately, chairs scooted closer, heads lowered and all the Simpsons asked questions at once. For more than an hour Ava told them about herself, trying to squeeze in her own questions about Arnie in between.

On the sidelines, Arnie watched proudly, listening to the chatter and smiling at her whenever their eyes met.

"So then Arnie got this scholarship to that school back east. We missed the runt, even though he caused a peck of trouble in his teens." Tiny reached over the table and ruffled Arnie's hair.

"He stole cars," Marty said.

"He did not!"

"Aw, that was just for fun," Arnie put in. "I'd hide them in the woods and see how long it took everyone to find them."

"He kept a notebook of the times," Ray added. "Who took the longest again?"

Arnie shook his head. "Don't remember."

Everyone got quiet for a minute, as if trying to call the memories back.

"So tell me," Ava joked during the lull. "Where in the world did you get Arnie? He's so different from you all."

"Where'd we get Arnie?" Nora roared. "That's the twenty-four thousand dollar question, isn't it, Momma?" She took a sip of cola and grinned.

"It sure is," Mrs. Simpson said. "Don't know what we'd have done if we never found him."

"Don't we know it, too," Myra said. "I'd not be married to Donny. Arnie introduced us."

"I got lost?" Arnie asked. He looked confused, like someone who'd been left out of the "in" joke.

"You never got lost, Son." Mr. Simpson said.

"But you said you found me."

"Sure, we did," Mrs. Simpson sang. "In the state park. In a beer cooler."

Arnie laughed. Ava laughed.

No one else laughed.

Her face fell and her heart plunged to her toes.

Oh no.

No.

"That's right, Mabel," Mr. Simpson said. "Good old Sputnik, the beer cooler. I'd forgotten all about that."

"Remember, Ted?" Mabel ran an affectionate hand along his five o'clock shadow. "Seems like Arnie's been ours forever."

The front legs of Arnie's chair crashed down. "You're serious?"

Ava launched a hand into his lap. He didn't respond.

"Sure, Son. You knew that."

"No, I did not!"

"You mean we never told you?"

"No!" Arnie bellowed. "I suggest I would remember!"

"He never asked," Mabel said to the table, dismissing Arnie's outrage with a small wave. "Lord knows he asked every other question under the sun—including how it got in the sky."

"Why I would I ask if you *found* me in a *beer cooler*?" Arnie barked, saucer-eyed. "Oh wait. I forgot. All kids ask that."

The Simpsons exchanged glances.

"Guess he's not as smart as he thinks," Tiny commented.

"He's one of those savants," Marty teased.

"Didn't you ever wonder why you looked different?" Ray asked.

Arnie's mouth opened and closed but nothing came out. Tiny sobs of air quaked Ava's chest. She squeezed his thigh—to remind him he had reinforcements. No one knew how he felt right now better than she.

"I never noticed until recently," he said weakly.

No one said anything, just stared at him. This was not only weird, it was cruel.

Suddenly, the atmosphere around him coiled and funneled. The powerful muscle in his thigh turned to iron beneath her fingers belying the softness of his tone.

"All of you knew?"

He met each of their eyes.

One by one.

And one by one they nodded.

All the way down the line.

* * * * *

For the first time in his life — except for those early hours with The Entity — Arnie felt like a complete and utter moron.

How could he have been so dopey? He was nothing like the siblings — any of them. For one thing, he was much shorter and for another, he had brains.

He gave his forehead a mental slug. *Used* to have brains. What was up there now, shit? He shook his head, trying to understand. "So you found me in the park and adopted me?" he asked, desperate for a foothold, a solid fact.

His mother frowned. "Oh no. We never adopted you officially."

"Then I'm not a Simpson?"

"You're a Simpson to us, Son," his father said.

A murmur of agreement traversed the table.

"But my parents abandoned me and you took me in." Arnie said it as more of a statement than a question.

"Something like that," his mother said.

"Something *like* that?"

She patted his hand. "Abandonment is a strong word, honey. We'd rather think of it like they forgot you."

"Forgot me?" Somewhere along the line, his brain had gone to instant replay. "That's better?"

"Well, maybe they didn't forget you—"

"Then what?" Arnie hollered. "What happened?"

His father took an exasperated breath, as if he'd reiterated the story a thousand times and Arnie just didn't get it. "Son, all we know is we found you alone in the woods. We didn't want to let a bear get you so we took you home. No one ever claimed you. So we raised you."

Arnie sagged in his chair. This was bad. He'd run out of the energy to bellow so he just asked quietly. "Did you ever call the police?"

"No, no," his mother put in. "They'd have put you in an orphanage. I wouldn't stand for that. Not when I had plenty of food for the table."

Off in a distant corner of his mind he told himself this wasn't happening, couldn't possibly be. Why did he not believe himself? Could he end this line of conversation now, tuck it away in a dark, unused spot of his mind and forget about it?

"You were such a cute spud. And you know how I get when I hold a baby," she said.

His dad patted her shoulder. "She'd just had a miscarriage and had that postpartum thing women get. I couldn't bear to take you away from her."

She had six others before him! Arnie held his tongue. "But what about my real parents," he asked. At her stricken look he amended, "My other parents?"

"What about them. They ran off, I guess."

"They never looked for me?"

"Not that we know of."

"Look, Son. We know it's hard," his father said. "They were probably young—"

"And they shouldn't have left you. Why, a bear could have gotten you," his mother reiterated.

That was true. Even in his astonishment Arnie saw the sense in that. "But a bear didn't get me. You got me and you should've given me back."

His father harrumphed, his mother let out a strangled cry, all the girls crossed their arms and the men comforted them. Only Tiny spoke. "That sounds awfully ungrateful."

"I didn't mean it that way!" Arnie shouted. He held a hand up to his face, pinching the bridge of his nose. "I'm confused."

Something in him made him ask the next question, even though he almost knew what the answer would be. "What about my birth certificate, my social security number?"

*My whole frickin identity?*

"Oh that," his mother waved. "Doc Hollis was old and grumpy. I just told him I lost your papers and he wrote me up some more. Since I had most of you at home, he lost count years before you came along."

So someone had left him in a cooler, in the woods, alone and misbegotten. Ted and Mabel happened along and he magically became Arnie Simpson, sphincter-extraordinaire.

How had he not realized it before?

All the times he'd asked a question at the dinner table only to see the chewing stop and all faces turn wide-eyed toward him. The hours Mabel would spend at her sewing machine tailoring Tiny's hand-me-downs for Arnie, only to turn around and undo it for Marty and Ray when it was their turn for the clothes.

His scholarships, their tractor loans. His plasma experiments, their paper airplanes.

The Observers…

But more than that, his chronic loneliness. Even in a family of twelve. He'd always felt frustrated, unable to communicate.

And now he felt…

*Alienated.*

Jumping up so violently his chair flew over, he flung himself through the crowd, jogged across the field and hopped into his car. Only as he fired the engine did he hear Ava shouting his name.

Did he want to see her right now, listen to her platitudes? He needed solitude, a chance to think things through. He couldn't do that if she was near, seducing him, bringing The Observers, making his mind even fuzzier.

So, pretending not to hear her desperate plea—though it nearly killed him to leave her—he gunned the engine and tore away from his family.

The only one he'd ever known.

# CHAPTER NINE

Once he'd arrived at the hangar and calmed down a bit, Arnie figured she'd come and she did. He didn't know whether to be upset or relieved when he heard the door slide open and her slender self slide inside.

All he knew was he needed her—even though he hadn't thought so—and she'd known. Whether her motivation came from a sense of possessiveness, her doctor's need to help, or out of love for him, hardly mattered. He didn't know who *him* was anymore.

He had a lot of work to do. He needed to know who his real parents were and reckoned it would be a long process, entailing weeks of research on the Internet, hours in libraries and police stations.

He had no idea how old he'd been when the Simpsons found him. His memory snippets went back to two. They'd mentioned they found him in an ice chest, which not only led to the conclusion he'd been too young to crawl out but also tied some new and scary suspicions into a permanent knot in his gut.

His father had mentioned Sputnik, the atomic-looking metal ice chest that'd featured in countless family picnics—one of those space-age relics from the fifties that'd go for big bucks on Internet auctions these days. Had that been the beer cooler they'd found him in? What had happened to it? Did one of the sibs still have it tucked away in a barn somewhere?

And did it look as much like a freakin' cryo tank as he remembered?

How ironic if all this time he blamed Ava for being the alien when, in fact, it was himself.

Arnie's whole body went numb and his brain sloshed in puddles of fear. Wouldn't be logical to jump to conclusions before all the evidence was in. The most important thing right now was that he finally had validation for some of the weirdness in his life. And, he had a starting point from which to research it.

"I'll help you," she said softly.

He looked up from the airplane, sucking in a breath at her beauty. Setting down his tool, he reached for her, burying his face in her neck, backing her into the office.

His arms came around her in a crushing embrace, forcing the air out of her lungs into his. Mouth opening over hers, he gulped her in, his hands tearing at her gown, getting her naked in record time. Ava yanked his trousers open, peeling them down to the floor. He hoisted her onto the desk, then up over him, taking her against it with great, pounding thrusts.

When they climaxed in a white-hot flash, pummeling, scratching and moaning, he relaxed against her, allowing one of her feet to slide to the floor, but keeping himself firmly inside.

Dropping his damp forehead onto hers, his gaze levered into hers. "I love you," he whispered.

Spending every last ounce of strength he had left with the admission, Arnie sank into her arms, dimly noting that if he'd lost one home tonight, he'd gained another in its stead.

*  *  *  *  *

"Since you slept at Arnie's, we stayed here at home last night instead of going to the lake," Lorna said over the phone the next morning. "We decided to postpone the honeymoon so we can help Arnie."

"You're going," Ava said firmly. "He doesn't want you to miss your honeymoon."

"We can do that anytime. And you need to go home tomorrow, so we'll stay for him."

Ava sighed. Home. Where was that now? Sometime during the last few days her concept of what constituted a home had shifted.

During her youth, Fairbanks was home. And she'd fled it as soon as she could. Up until this week, she considered Minneapolis home. Still did.

But not without Arnie.

A voice she scarcely recognized as her own said, "I'm not going until he finds out who his birth parents are."

It could take days, weeks, years. But Ava's heart ached for him. Where had *his* home gone? Children were supposed to leave it, not have it leave them.

There was a silence on the other end of the phone. "You're not leaving?"

Ava swallowed hard, her breathing suddenly labored, pulse quickening. "Not yet," she croaked. *What was she doing?*

"I can't believe you just said that."

"It's temporary."

"This is huge. Gage!"

"Stop. Please. Don't yell for Gage."

"Of course I'm yelling for Gage. He's my husband. Gage! She's staying."

Ava yanked the receiver from her ear and pressed it tightly to her breast, taking a huge gulp of air before lifting the receiver again. "Lorna, listen. I'm not going to live here."

"She says she's going to live here."

"I'm just taking emergency leave to care for Arnie."

"She cares for Arnie."

"Stop lying to Gage! This is serious." Ava rested her forehead against the wall, rocking it slowly in frustration.

"Okay. Okay." Lorna backed off.

An inch away from Ava's eyes, the wall looked rough. She could spot all the bumps in the drywall. Funny how it looked so smooth from far away. Life had the same problem, she thought. It didn't bear close inspection. "Arnie needs me."

"I know."

"I'm tired of putting job before family." Her contract with Dr. Linus provided three months' emergency leave and in Ava's estimation, this qualified. Although she still didn't know what they would do about future living arrangements, she was unequivocally hooked up with Arnie now, for as long as he'd have her. "But I'm never, I repeat never, going to live here."

*Am I?*

"I hear ya."

Ava glanced inside the bedroom. As soon as they got home last night, they'd headed for bed. She'd awakened early, concern for him resulting in a restless night, and had called Lorna from the hallway telephone to explain everything.

"He told me he loved me," Ava said, realizing she'd been in doctor mode and failed to return the sentiment. She seriously needed lessons for relating on a personal level. She'd ventured into uncharted territory with this thing called love.

"Duh," Lorna answered.

"So we're fine here. Go on your honeymoon."

From Ava's end, it sounded like Lorna was rapidly tapping a pencil on her desk. Ava knew that meant she was thinking. Plotting.

"Okay, we'll get ready and call you before we take off in case of any last-minute changes. Let me know as soon as you find out who these mystery people are. I'll have my cell with me. Do you have my number? I got a new plan when I moved here."

Ava took a minute to jot down Lorna's number, leaving the note on the telephone table, then hung up and went back to Arnie.

"Where'd you go?" he asked sleepily when she crawled in next to him. The sheets were tangled and knotted around his legs, evidence of his unspoken distress. Ava took a moment to neaten them.

"Talking to Lorna," she said. "Want me to bring you breakfast in bed?"

"Yeah," he murmured, cracking an eyelid.

"Coming right up."

As she vaulted off the bed, Arnie reached out and grabbed her, yanking her down and rolling on top. His sleep-warmed, silky skin enveloped her, the clean masculine scent of him making her woozy.

"No need to go all the way in the kitchen for my meal," he said. "I suggest I have an appetite for what I see right here."

His lips headed south down her body, nibbling and sucking on the hills and valleys along the road. The velvety-soft texture of his mouth wrapped her heart in a fuzzy fleece blanket of security while the tickly delight of his hair and the scratch of his unshaven chin stimulated and quickened the nerves along her skin.

With his tongue, he dabbed each crest of hipbone, drawing a lazy line across her stomach to connect them and pausing for a moment in the crevice of her bellybutton.

"Hey, you have an outie," he muttered.

"It used to be worse. Almost like a third nipple. I hated it."

"I wonder if it's as sensitive." He jabbed it with the tip of his tongue as if testing the theory. Then he caught the slight nub in his teeth and gently nipped.

Arrows of pleasure-pain shot out at every angle, slicing through her abdomen, nicking her brain and piercing her heart. How many other men had perceived her body as a playground, a science lab *and* a sports arena? Uh. None. And there'd never be another like Arnie again.

With one deft shot, he'd hit every emotional target she owned, bull's-eye. Now he was taking aim again. Ava threaded her fingers through his hair as he nuzzled between her legs, hearing his muffled sounds of pleasure when he tasted the sweets he found.

His darting tongue slammed her to the apex in about thirty seconds and just when she dangled on the edge of the precipice, he reared up and thrust himself inside. The resulting torrent surged through her in two shattering orgasms, one inner and one outer. Her entire being exploded with a fullness it could no longer contain as the genital shocks from one and the total body blowout from the other ate her alive.

"Arnie," she shouted, bucking helplessly beneath him. "I love you. I love you."

She chanted it over and over, tears seeping from her eyes. And the act of reciting those words while her body thrummed to his beat intensified the passion she felt for him until she was struck dumb.

In the hollow of silence her muteness left, Arnie picked up the note, singing it himself until he too shuddered in a climax that heaved them skyward.

They rolled on the mattress like wrestlers, her legs locked around his plunging hips, his arms cinched around her buttocks. The intensity of the aftershocks nearly vaporized them. When they finally grew still, the heaviness of their breathing formed a thick and teeming vortex of infatuation around the bed.

But they refused to unlatch. She wiggled on the axis of his cock and pressed its solid head up firmly against her back wall. The super-sensitized flesh inside her pussy sucked along each ridge, memorizing him by touch and engraving that memory at cellular level in her body.

His thrusts slowed to one or two a minute, but each time, they both quivered. At last, one final release gyroed through his body like a dog shaking off water and they slumped on the pillows, spent and exhausted.

"You love me?" Arnie asked against her breast.

She let her words drift out on a dreamy sigh. "I adore you." Somehow, he'd always been part of her. The undiscovered part. And here she'd thought she'd known herself so well.

He reared up on his arms, lifting his face to the ceiling and turned loose a primitive, lilting howl.

Ava fell apart laughing.

"I suggest we get married soon," Arnie said, flopping back down. He twirled a strand of her hair and absently tickled her nipple with it. "I waited long enough for you. Got to strike while the iron's hot."

She grabbed a fistful of his hair and gently pulled his face up. "Did you just ask me to marry you?"

He shook his head somberly, taking the strand of hair and painting her lower lip. "I didn't ask. I suggested."

Ava pushed them both upright until they were sitting. Resting an elbow on the pillow behind him, she put on her doctor face. "What is it with you and your suggestions?" She poked him gently with her index finger.

Tenderly, he laced his fingers through hers, brought her hand to his lips and kissed it. She scooted closer, coasting her free hand down his shoulder. "Promise not to tell?"

Ava cocked her head. "Tell what?"

He chuckled. "People are almost hypnotized by the word 'suggest'. They'll do or believe almost anything if you suggest it rather than say it."

Ava's jaw dropped. Edging onto his lap, she couldn't help but giggle. "You mean to tell me all this time I thought you were being polite, you were actually manipulating people?"

"I suggest I wouldn't go that far."

"Arnie Simpson, I'm shocked." She wagged a finger under his nose. "You've been a very bad boy."

He grinned wickedly. "I suggest I should be punished."

"I suggest I agree."

"Then marry me," he said, lunging forward and capturing her wrists before she could swat him. "Trust me, that'll be punishment enough."

Ava opened her mouth to bellow so he kissed her. Bucking against him in playful anger, she felt the liquid heat of desire start simmering in her loins again. Best to stop now before things got out of hand. Again.

"We'll talk it over," she said noncommittally, pushing him gently away. She hated the treacherous thoughts creeping into her mind. But the idea that Arnie proposed because he'd experienced a catastrophic emotional upheaval had already grown tenacious roots. He'd been cast adrift and needed a lifeboat. Wouldn't you know she'd be sailing right behind?

"What do you mean, *we'll talk it over*?"

"What do you mean what do I mean? We'll talk about it."

"When?"

"Soon."

"What are you trying to say?" he asked in a strangled voice.

"Shh." She pressed two fingers to his lips. "Before you even think about where we're going, you have to find out where you came from."

"That's not going to change anything."

"I'm not saying it will—"

"Unless you're worried about some genetic disease."

"Will you stop? That's the farthest thing from my mind. I'm just saying you have a lot going on in your head right now and you need to handle one thing at a time."

"I suggest I could multi-task."

"I'm sure you could."

"I'm not some idiot who can't figure out he was a foundling."

Ava pulled back. This was good. He was starting to display. He needed to get all that rage out in order to begin the healing process. "No, you're not an idiot. Is that how you feel?"

Arnie slammed his palm on the mattress. "You saw what happened. How do you think I feel?"

She curled up next to him. "I would imagine angry, for starters."

He fumed silently, drumming his fingers on the bedside table. "I don't know how I feel," he finally said. "Believe me, I'd tell you if I did."

Ava sighed deeply. "I'm here. I'll help you."

"You're just saying that because you're a doctor and you hate to see people suffer."

"That's only partly true. I also happen to love you."

He pinned her with fiery eyes. "Then marry me."

"Arnie—"

"Now."

"Arnie." She reached out to stroke his face. He grabbed her hand and held on, a wild, desperate look on his face.

He stared at her for a long time, plunging into her mind, finding something he didn't like, and letting her hand drop. "Right," he said, tumbling her off his lap and springing from the bed.

She scrambled to her knees. "Where are you going?"

He spun around, anger etched on his face. "To take a shower."

"Can I join you?" she asked.

"Not this time," he snarled, pounding down the stairs.

Great. Just great! Ava punched his pillow until feather dust billowed around her head. *You handled that one with aplomb, Miss Bedside Manner. How ham-handed could you get?*

But there was no backing down. When she married Arnie, she wanted to go into it with complete assurance she wasn't merely a replacement for the family he felt estranged from and for the one he'd never known. She needed to be clear on the fact that he loved her, not just needed her. How else could she be secure in their future?

\* \* \* \* \*

Arnie smacked a fist against the tile wall of the shower, standing under the spray, trying to wash away his devastation. He would've cracked open his chest and let the hot water course through if there'd been a chance of soothing the black-and-blue bruise where his heart once beat.

He bellowed, punching the wall again. How could she love him and not ache to marry, as he did? Wasn't that the logical progression? Women were always yapping about marriage. He'd fielded enough relationships to have a keen bead on that.

Her desire to locate his breeders beforehand was nothing but a bunch of bullshit, a lame attempt to string him along. Despite her actions of last night, she still saw him as a diversion.

His heart plunged to the pit of his stomach with the splintering suction of a splashdown. Now he knew for sure love existed. And it most certainly bit the big one.

He emerged from the shower, lathering up and savagely shaving. Who cared if his mug got shredded to a bloody, pussy pulp? He scrubbed his teeth furiously, managed to stave off gingivitis for another day and, not bothering to comb his wet hair, stalked back to the bedroom where Ava sat nervously on the bed.

"I heard you yelling in the shower," she said.

"Yeah? So what."

"You have every right to be angry."

"Thanks for validating me."

"Arnie, don't do this. Don't blame me. Your parents—"

"They're not my parents!" he spewed. "They're monsters. What kind of animals wouldn't even make an effort to find a lost baby's family?"

"I don't know," she whispered.

"Is that sick or am I nitpicking?"

She shrugged her shoulders in a helpless, vague way. "They loved you too."

"Love? For thirty-four years they let me believe I was their son, and then made me feel like an idiot for not figuring out I wasn't. You call that love?" Arnie punched his legs into his jeans. "If you believe that, you really are an alien."

Ava flinched as if struck. The action brought him a flicker of sorrow, but his own misery quickly welled back up to overwhelm it.

She vocalized again. "I know it sounds strange. I'm trying to understand too."

"Don't do me any favors." His bitterness toward her for the minor piece of him she wanted rose like bile in his throat.

"In a way, it's a compliment. They thought you were smart enough to realize you were adopted."

"Listen." Arnie got right in her face, making her rear back in fear. "I wasn't adopted. From what it sounds like, I was abducted." And it also sounded like no one ever checked up on him. No police, no parents. Nobody. They would've easily found him if they had.

He was alone.

He had to get out of here, was rabidly enraged, confused, crazy in love and worst of all, on the verge of blubbering.

The stinging pressure mounting behind his eyes drove him from the house as Ava shouted his name. He shot the Porsche through town without the slightest inkling where to go. Where could he go? Where the hell could he go to pummel the holy living shit out of something and bawl like a frickin' baby while he did it?

Blindly, he circled back toward the farm.

The trail of dust billowing up the driveway to Tiny's house must have alerted the pseudo-brothers to his approach. Marty, Ray and Tiny stood shoulder to shoulder like a wall when he leaped out of the car.

"Been expecting you, runt, let's see what you got," Tiny challenged, monstrous hands banking his hips. The other two braced him for impact. Like giant Redwoods they absorbed and deflected his banshee fury, allowing him blow after stinging blow.

"You a man or a mouse?" Tiny huffed, egging him on. "Is that all?"

"No!" He pummeled some more. "They were wrong to leave me."

"Maybe. Maybe not."

"I don't know who I am."

"You don't. But we do."

Arnie slumped. As suddenly as he started, he stopped, depleted, and weaved tiredly into the house.

The brothers watched him disappear before breaking out in muffled moans. Bending low in the agony they'd bottled, they quietly compared cuts and bruises.

"That little scamp can fight," Tiny groaned.

"I hope you stocked up on ice packs," Marty grimaced.

"Just point me to the whiskey," Ray winced.

With grudging admiration, Marty and Ray limped into the kitchen, hauled out a cold case, sat down at the table and parked an icy six-pack under their big brother's nose.

Arnie chugged the first three in about sixty seconds while Tiny scrounged in the back bedroom. By the time he returned with a bulging folder, Arnie was on his fourth beer and feeling considerably brighter about his predicament. "What's that?" he belched.

"Found someone who might know a little about who you are and where you came from." Tiny grinned and opened the folder. "Stayed up all night surfing the Internet. But before I tell you what I found, take a gander at this."

Arnie focused blearily on the yellowed newspaper clipping Tiny placed in front of him. Shaking his head clear, he bent closer for a better look at the headline—*UFOs in Flintlock?*

The article was dated nineteen-seventy-two and outlined the details of a mysterious object seen hovering in the sky. As his brain registered key words in the article, a cold hand squeezed his heart. "What does this have to do with me?" So some nut had seen a flying saucer over the park where he was found. Big deal. Happened all the time.

Tiny popped the lid off a beer and took a long gulp. "Well, a day after Momma brought you home, this article appeared in the paper. I saw it at Billy's house. His dad took all the Madison papers."

Arnie nodded.

"I just always wondered. Seemed like a weird coincidence. But I never did anything about it. What happened at the wedding got me to remembering, so last night after we got back, I went and researched."

Tiny'd done that? For him? Arnie studied the big lunk. "What'd you find?" Scientific curiosity converged with abject terror and took over for the moment, allowing him to step back and listen to the evidence. If nothing else, it'd make a great story to tell his friends at the E.T. Institute.

"I instant-messaged with some of your cronies at E.T. Turns out there's a whole mess of information about this particular sighting."

Would wonders never cease? Yeah. Four beers felt good right about now. "How come I never heard about it, then?"

Tiny looked at him. "How long since you searched current events at E.T.? This information was uncovered a few months ago when a Rockwell engineer donated his personal journal to the institute."

He hadn't been in touch for a while. Arnie's heart started pounding. "I suggest you go on."

"Well, in a nutshell seems this engineer was involved with the Apollo Thirteen project and worked on the forensic investigation of the service module debris afterward. The one you're obsessed with." Tiny paused, as if for validation.

Arnie's head bobbed. Apollo Thirteen's problems and his inability to independently solve them had followed him like a bad fart his whole life. Was, in fact, the reason he never went into aerospace engineering. Who'd want a dodo like him trying to bring a crippled rocket ship back from certain doom? But Tiny'd gotten some bad information. "There wasn't any debris."

"Maybe that's the public story," Tiny continued. "And here's the reason they might've not wanted tell the real one. Seems the engineer found something in a chunk of fuselage — in the hole that got blasted out of it. Or into it. Seems that something was a cryogenic tank with a see-through lid." He stopped, pressed his lips tight then opened them. "It contained a life form."

Was his big brother slurring his words or did Arnie just hear them that way?

"A frozen baby."

Did his brain just get vacuumed out?

"The engineer took it and hid it because he was afraid the government would dissect the frozen baby — which appeared human to him. This tank had a black box recorder and for several months the engineer plugged it into the Rockwell computers in his spare time, trying to break the space code and get the thing to open up. Or at least trying to find out what the frick happened and how this thing got lodged inside the Apollo service module."

It sounded like Tiny had stuck his head into a fish tank and was talking to the creatures he found inside. No way was he talking to Arnie.

"He never managed to decipher the language from the recorder but he developed a couple of theories based on the technology of the tank. One, that aliens put it on board while the module was on the other side of the moon, to get it here, as in maybe they couldn't get it here on their own. Two, that an alien ship was in distress and fortuitously encountered the module and stuck the tank in there before crashing—maybe even causing the explosion that threatened the astronauts."

Arnie stared at the imaginary fish tank and remembered the burnt smell of last night. Some keen emotion sprouted in his soul and, oddly enough, made him want to turn backflips. It felt like…

"Either way, seems Apollo Thirteen was a miraculous story in more than one way."

*Joy.* The air in the room started sloshing and the fish started swimming inside Arnie's eyeballs.

"Finally, the dang thing started bleeping. Like an alarm going off. Or a time bomb. Or, a distress signal.

"The engineer took it out to the country and sat back to watch and see what happened. At this point he didn't think there was anything further he could do. Well, turns out he'd done the right thing. It was a distress signal. A spaceship showed up, took the baby and the tank and disappeared. He said it was the most fearsome thing he'd ever seen. Said he went home with wet pants and didn't stop leaking for another five years after that. Bet he got irradiated so badly he didn't need a night light either." Tiny grinned at his own joke. "You got to talk to this guy."

Arnie's response mechanism got hopelessly scrambled.

"Anyway, the next day he read about twin UFO sightings—one in California, where he was, and one here in Flintlock. He never knew what it meant or what happened to the frozen baby he'd taken care of for two years. He was always afraid to talk about it, afraid he'd lose his job and his reputation. But now he's retired, rich and old and figures he can say whatever the hell he wants. He also wants to find the baby. Says he thinks of him like a son."

Arnie snorted. Or like a pet turtle, most likely.

"The NASA geeks are maintaining he's demented. Said he always was a little spacey. And maybe he is. But ole Tiny thinks there might be something to this." He paused meaningfully. "What do you think?"

From somewhere in The Deep, Arnie found his words. "Need. To. Call. The-men-in-white-coats." Tiny had to be crazy. Yet, his words had a resonance of truth that echoed like a sweet, high note through all the empty caverns of Arnie's being.

"Then take a look." Tiny shoved a grainy black-and-white picture under his nose.

"Sputnik. The beer cooler," Arnie stuttered. *With a baby inside*. "Mabel and Ted took a picture when they found me?" Hey, sanity was worth one last shot.

"Guess again. This photo was taken by the engineer. It's the cryo tank. And that's you. I'd recognize you anywhere."

Unfettered excitement and an unexpected, exquisite sense of hope clobbered him so hard he had to grip the sides of his chair.

"The engineer's name is Robert Walker. He and his wife called you Michael. After the Archangel. Wanna know why?"

Hadn't one of the Observers told Ava that *Michael's* destiny rested with her? "Why?" he croaked.

"'Cause in their hearts they believe you guarded those astronauts and helped them get home."

\* \* \* \* \*

Twin jackhammers machine-gunning his temples greeted him the next day as he struggled to sit up and figure out where he was.

Shitake Mushrooms! He slumped back down, massaging his head and trying not to scream. He opened one eye between throbs, recognizing the gray and brown train track pattern on Marty's decrepit sofa.

How'd he get here? He recalled raising Cain at the Hangaround last night with his brothers, glugging mugs of beer and sidecars of whiskey. Somewhere along the line they'd led everyone in a rousing rendition of the song "Aliens Are Dancing on the Milky Way", but the rest was a blur. He just hoped he didn't embarrass himself by taking a ride on the vomit comet.

Ignoring the acid-induced nightmare Marty called wallpaper, Arnie plodded into the bathroom and dug around for aspirin. Weaving into the kitchen, he opened the fridge, nearly lost it at the surge of rotten fumes and checked the expiration date on the orange juice. Last May, only two months. Arnie weighed the benefits of potassium replenishment against the odds of agonizing death, took a risk and swallowed pills and poison.

Marty seriously needed to get married.

For that matter, so did Arnie.

Ava!

He spun from the fridge and checked the clock. High noon. His ass was grass. Leaving a blue streak of epithets in his wake, he galloped the quarter mile to Tiny's house and hopped in the speedster. With a wrench of gears, he lurched into a one-eighty and rocketed to his house.

In the light of day and with this new information about his heritage, the anger he felt had vanished into thin air.

Despite Tiny's fantastical theory, and Arnie's completely dopey desire to believe it, cool logic had returned and he'd concluded Robert Walker was most likely his biological father, and had most likely gone cuckoo. *Most likely*.

Perhaps both his biological parents had been too young to take care of him. Perhaps they weren't married. Whatever. The upshot was they left him in the park as an infant. Intentionally. Without looking back.

No way was he an alien.

*Stop wishing you were, moron.*

There was no logic in that, even though it would be too cool for words.

*Why hope for the improbable?*

Every one of his vital functions appeared human, except for the mood eyes and the strange interiors of his mind—which was par for the course for a nerd. A DNA cheek swab would confirm it. *Unfortunately.*

With his internal network of connections through ETI he figured he could have an answer in days. He put it on his immediate To Do list.

Eventually, he'd get in touch with the madman and find out what really happened. But for now, simply suspecting an Apollo engineer's blood ran in his veins, that his probable father believed in him and trusted his abilities to save the day, was enough to make him look at himself in a new light.

Because of this, the thought of working in an office with other geeks—geeks who might be even smarter than him—didn't seem quite so threatening anymore. Besides, he'd have to do *something* responsible with his life if he wanted to get married and start a family with Ava. He wanted to be a fruitful example for the offspring, and he wanted his wife's respect.

Unfortunately, he'd probably put a crack in any budding respect by acting like a crazed bully, venting his rage at her when she was trying to help.

And she'd been right. He wouldn't have been able to make a sensible decision about what to have for breakfast, let alone who to marry, with all those emotions churning butter in his brain.

He only hoped it wasn't too late to tell her.

Bursting into his living room, a chunk of his heart broke off when he sensed right away she was gone. The house had that breathless, hollow calm. Pounding upstairs to make sure, his eye caught a note on the hallway phone table. Lorna's cell phone number. Dialing frantically, he hoped he'd catch them at the lake and see if they'd heard from Ava.

"Hello?" Lorna said.

"It's Arnie," he barked.

"It's Arnie," he heard her tell Gage. *Tell him to come over*, he heard Gage say.

"We just got home," Lorna said. "Why don't you…"

He smacked down the phone, dread seeping into every pore. They'd just gotten home. From the lake? If they came home early that meant an emergency.

Racing to their house, all his fears collided into a teeming vortex of agony. Ava couldn't be dead. He discarded that one. Hurt? Maybe. Before he could hurtle further along that ghastly tunnel, he arrived.

Gage met him at the door, another ominous sign. Halfway up the walk Arnie froze in his tracks. "Where is she?" He wasn't about to waste time chatting if she was in the hospital.

"Minneapolis," Gage said. "We took her to the airport this morning. She's probably home by now."

Relief that she still breathed Earth air flooded through him, nearly buckling his knees. He would've gone back to Marty's and injected the rest of the orange juice otherwise.

"You're all they can talk about at the airport," Gage added. "Some money changed hands from long-standing bets."

Arnie threw him a grin. "Stranger than science fiction. I'll tell you more when you get back from Canada…" A terrible realization slammed him. "Your honeymoon!"

Gage waved a hand in dismissal. "Changed plans. Gonna drive up tomorrow."

"You're gonna drive?" Gage never crawled when he could soar. Totally out of character.

"I thought up a better use for the Mooney." Gage dug into his pocket and tossed him The Keys. Arnie caught them and looked down at them. Stark fear weighted them in his palm. "I can't"

"Sure, you can. You have to. Don't have a choice."

They got heavier in his hand, like a toddler becoming deadweight on the floor when it didn't want to be picked up, as heavy as the bond he had with his brothers, with Gage. As heavy as his love for Ava. He looked back up and his voice cracked. "I have to find something out before I go get her. Something that might change things between us."

Lorna had materialized, smiling, in the doorway. "Nothing's going to change. No matter what. Ava loves you, you know," she said.

He swallowed. Hard. Without realizing it, he'd needed that assurance from Lorna. And she'd given it. "I love her. And I love you two pinheads." He could do this. He could. So why wouldn't his legs work?

*Make them.* If he turned his shoulders back toward the car, his hips and legs would follow. An object in motion tended to stay in motion. So all he had to do was start moving. Sounded simple enough.

Until every phobia known to mankind dropped and rolled into his colon and threatened to break for it if he didn't keep his legs locked together.

"Go," Gage growled. "Time's a wasting."

"I'm going. I'm going."

"You're gonna have to do it a little faster or I might change my mind again."

"Bullshit." It was a thinly veiled manipulation and Arnie knew it, but it had the desired effect on his body. As if on autopilot his hips swiveled and the legs began trotting to the speedster. Hopping into the car, he glanced back at the happy couple.

Gage grinned. "Godspeed, Michael Walker."

# CHAPTER TEN

Seven days later, Ava had begun the arduous process of severing ties with Dr. Linus. There was simply no way she could live in Minneapolis if it meant living without Arnie, but she hadn't realized that until he'd left her and she'd come home. Alone.

After he'd stormed out, she'd caught Lorna and Gage before they left and cried on Lorna's shoulder all afternoon — deciding she couldn't care less what he did for a living. It no longer mattered if he wanted to tinker on toy planes for the rest of his life. As long as he came home to her at night.

Even in Flintlock.

She shuddered. The path she'd chosen scared the bejeezus out of her. But she saw no other way. She couldn't ask him to leave his hometown, not now, maybe not ever. Since she couldn't bring him to her, she'd have to go to him.

Hadn't Tiny said Flintlock needed a proctologist? Ava knew if Tiny became a patient, the rest of the town would follow. She'd be a small-town doc before she knew it.

But she would never lose her edge.

Ava's throat closed at the memory of her father on his deathbed. He never blamed the doctor, never gave it a second thought. It was Ava who'd pointed the finger all these years. Now she realized she wouldn't fall into that trap no matter where she lived. She'd take classes, read journals, attend conferences. It would mean some time on the road away from Arnie, but the alternative, life without him, was unthinkable.

If she ever got the chance to tell him.

Her doctor side chided her to relax. She'd had plenty of psych courses, could fully empathize, if not sympathize, with the trauma he'd experienced.

But on a personal side, her heart ached like the dickens. What if he never pulled out of his grief? What if her presence became indelibly entwined with his agonizing sorrow at the reception, and he transferred all those horrid feelings onto her — as he'd appeared to do the following morning?

She'd heard the fury in his voice, seen his distant expression, felt his icy withdrawal. Gone were the passionate, swirling brimstone eyes that had swept her away. They'd turned to cold hard stone from the hurt.

So she'd decided to give him some space, thinking it was for the best. Everything had happened so quickly, perhaps they both needed time to breathe.

Yeah, right. Like she did.

The bleep of the intercom in her office startled her out of her daydream. "Yes, Bonnie?" she asked the receptionist.

"I just got a visit from a new patient. He's coming back tonight, last appointment."

"Oh, yeah?" Ava's interest perked up. Bonnie only mentioned new patients when she saw something funny about them. Ava could use a good laugh right now.

"Well, he's kinda young," Bonnie said. "And a real hottie."

From the end she'd be inspecting, it was doubtful she'd notice. "What's your point?"

"Under symptoms, he listed pilonidal cyst but he spelled it *pillow nerdal cyst*."

Ava tittered, shrugging. So he was an illiterate hottie with enough medical knowledge to self-diagnose. Unusual, but not abnormal.

"There's another symptom written there."

Ava sighed impatiently. "Yes, Bonnie?" The girl could yak when she got in the mood.

"He wrote 'blue balls'," Bonnie snickered, proud of her punch line.

Great. A joker. Certain types got embarrassed by erectile dysfunction and sometimes laid that humiliation at her feet in the form of crude jokes. She wasn't really in the mood for it tonight, but oh well. Came with the territory.

He sounded high-maintenance, meaning closing time would be pushed back. Okay by her. The less time she had to spend alone in her townhouse the better.

"Bring me his chart."

She spent the rest of the evening seeing patients, catching up on paperwork and trying to get past the dread building in her heart with each passing hour. Couldn't Arnie at least call?

Several times in the past week she'd picked up the phone to call him, only to slam it back down after the first ring. Something in her rebelled at the idea of begging him to take her back. Then there was the fear of hearing icebergs calving in his voice. And dammit! She wanted him to call her. He owed it to her after what had happened.

Wondering how much longer she'd be able to endure his silence, she headed to her office for a break.

Relaxing a few minutes with a cup of coffee and an ice pack for her head, she picked up the new patient form and idly flipped through it.

Michael Walker, age—thirty-four, occupation—Astrobiologist. Her heart did a pirouette. This man researched other life forms for a living? She'd never met one of those!

Intrigued, she scanned farther down, seeking the symptoms Bonnie had outlined. *Pillow Nerdal*. She laughed, finding it funnier this time around. It sounded like something Arnie'd dream up.

Best not to go there.

Hmm. At Mr. Walker's age, she'd probably wind up packing him off to an urologist for the blue balls—er, erectile dysfunction—but it always paid to err on the side of caution.

Being a scientist, he'd probably thought of that himself and was merely covering his bases.

Admirable trait.

Neatening her white lab coat, she strode down the hallway to Mr. Walker's examining room fully intent on mentioning her hobby during the examination. She was always grateful to find a topic of conversation to ease the tension and to have an astrobiologist turn up in her examining room was exciting indeed.

Rapping twice on the door, she didn't wait for an invitation to sweep inside, immediately turning to close it before facing him.

"I'm Ava Ward," she said, whirling into an empty room.

Strong arms ensnared her from behind and yanked her back against a powerful chest.

"Bonnie," she bellowed before a hand clamped over her mouth. She struggled against him, some part of her brain registering the familiar scent of this stranger. About to drive her heel into his instep, she froze at the sound of his voice.

"I suggest you allow me to introduce myself before calling in the SWAT team."

"Arnie," she whispered, swiveling around to lock lips with him, sagging into his crushing embrace.

He backed her up to the examining table, hoisting her bottom onto the paper-covered top. She wrapped her legs around his waist, binding him to her as if her life depended on it. "You came back to me."

"But in a different form," he joked, lifting his head to peer into her eyes. "I missed you." He touched his forehead down on hers, one of his many habits she cherished.

"Oh, God, I missed you too. I was so afraid you wouldn't…" Before she knew it she was trembling, all over, her voice stalling with thick emotion.

"Stop there." He petted her hair. "Never be afraid I won't come back."

For a few moments, they clasped each other in silence. There were no words for the joy in her heart anyway. She'd just have to show him how much he meant to her.

Smoothing her hands down his arms and breathing in that spicy, manly smell she adored, she paused, looking at him sharply. "Michael Walker?" *Michael.* The déjà vu center in her brain sparked. Nothing came to mind, though. She'd have to revisit that later.

"In the flesh." He spread his arms wide. "But you can call me Arnie."

She swept a gaze up and down his precious body. Something was different. It took her a minute to process. Omigod. He had on a shirt and tie. Something inside her revolted at the idea of her Arnie looking so polished, so…professional.

"Take me home," she said, barreling off the table and knocking him backwards. Tears welled in her eyes. "I need to get you out of those ridiculous clothes."

"I bet you say that to all your patients."

"Let's go." She turned and he grabbed her hand, meshing fingers and stroking them seductively.

"What's wrong with right here?"

"Oh no you don't—"

He yanked her back to the examining table. "Try and stop me," he growled, before opening her lab coat and eating her up with his hands.

"Stop," she half giggled. But he was already unbuttoning her pants, sliding them off, and returning to do the same to her blouse.

"Turn around and bend over," he said. "Time for a taste of your own medicine."

"Oh God."

*Do you want me there?*

"Yes."

*Good, because I was just asking to make you think you had a choice.*

Before she knew it he had her sprawled face first on the table, one hand kneading her ass. The whir of his zipper as it descended made her suddenly wet. He gently pulled her back over his cock, lubricated it thoroughly with her cream and eased the tip into the tight, puckered opening above her cunt. "Careful," she cautioned. "Go slowly please. This is new to me."

"Am I hurting you?"

"No." Surprisingly, it didn't feel *that* different from the other way. Must be some major nerve-endings in there and as long as she didn't resist, his entry was far more pleasurable than she ever would've guessed.

Time to add anal sex to her menu of regular activities.

He palmed her cunt, gently hooking his fingers inside her pussy and collecting more lubrication. She felt him spreading it the length of his shaft. Fractured gasps escaped them both as he pushed farther in and Ava felt the warm, sticky slap of his testicles against her pussy. The fullness of his cock in such an unlikely place made her nerves thrum steadily in anticipation.

"Everything seems to check out on this end," Arnie said, his voice thick with building strain. His nimble fingers played with her clitoris as he moved and she arched into them. He slid his thumb inside her vagina and pressed against her G-spot, cupping her pubic bone firmly and massaging both areas at once. Hot electrical charges began snapping and arcing in blue ribbons across her skin.

She watched them with a curious detachment. In the reflection off the stainless steel cabinets she noticed she and Arnie were encompassed in a vivid blue halo that filled the room. While she stared, other shapes began to swirl and take form within the halo. Misty male and female humanoid figures emerged and started grasping at each other. Within seconds she and Arnie were surrounded by people writhing in sexual ecstasy—against the wall, on the floor, hunched on the counters—scores of people engaging in a frenzied orgy of monumental proportion.

And all of them watching each other.

She met the passion-drugged eyes of the men and women, saw their faces ignite with fresh lust as they focused on hers, their bodies moving together faster, harder and their muscles bunching in mounting bliss.

Together, she and Arnie competed for Best of Show, each of his thrusts matching her heart, beat for beat. His quintessentially alpha reclamation of her body and soul sent them barreling into the maelstrom of extreme carnality, the sounds of lust and animal sex and the pinpricks of electricity against her flesh igniting her body and mind into white-hot incandescence.

*Feet don't fail me now.*

Too late. Her knees buckled and Arnie hoisted her up by her ass, bracing her against the table by leaning over her back. He grasped a breast in one hand and squeezed her sensitive nipple, completing the circuit to her clitoris and causing her to cry out as she climaxed in short, sharpened jolts.

With a fizzle and a pop, the heated halo burst, the blue electrical arcs sputtered and everyone disappeared.

Ava lay gasping on the table and wondered if the weirdness would ever end. Surely someday they'd be able to make love in peace. Alone. *Quietly.*

Her exhausted chuckle broke the sudden stillness.

"Somehow, you giggling while my cock is up your ass doesn't make me feel manly," Arnie griped. But she heard a smile in his voice.

"Wasn't laughing at you," she panted. "The Others were in full bloom."

"Were they?" He slipped out of her and went to wash up.

"You didn't see them?"

"Not this time. I was concentrating too hard. Didn't want to lose it."

Suddenly she realized he hadn't shared completely in the orgasmic experience. Twisting to face him, she glanced into devilish eyes. "Why?"

He zipped his fly and returned to her, pushing a damp lock of hair off her forehead. "I'm conserving my energy."

She arched a brow.

"I want to celebrate one week of knowing you, and make you come twice for each day you've made me the happiest geek on the planet."

"You're going to drive me insane."

"I'd rather drive you home. Get dressed."

Throwing on her clothes, she grabbed his tie, yanking him out of the examining room and down the hall. She pulled him into the reception area like a dog on a leash, startling Bonnie so badly she jumped.

"Mr. Walker is coming home with me," she said to her open-mouthed employee. "Lock up, will you?"

Bonnie nodded, staring at Arnie.

"Don't look at me," he said. "I suggest Dr. Ava decided to take my blue balls into her own hands."

Bonnie gave a strangled yelp. Ava hurtled him out the door.

Laughing uncontrollably, they raced her red BMW back to her townhouse in record time. Barely making it inside the threshold, they tore at each other, popping buttons, shredding underwear. Clothing hung off them like scarecrows as they dropped, writhing, to the floor.

The clock struck midnight about the same time Ava's legs failed. Arnie's knees were raw, so she padded into the bathroom for salve. Greasing him up while he sipped a cold beer and smacked his lips with pleasure, she said, "So tell me all about yourself, Michael."

Arnie snorted beer through his nose, the second time she'd made him do that. He sopped up the mess with a towel. "Remind me not to drink around you."

She listened while he told her who he thought his birth parents were, the new respect he had for his brothers and how they'd helped him. He seemed to choose his words slowly and carefully, as if editing them while he spoke, and she got the feeling she wasn't getting the whole story. But she let it slide. He'd tell her everything when he felt ready and if he wanted to keep a few private memories of an intensely personal journey, who was she to forbid him?

"I saw my folks before I came here," he said, lying on her bed, his chest pillowing her head. "I told them I was okay with it, even though I'm not. Heck, they're old. I'm not going to punish them. Besides, I suggest they raised me right."

"They sure did," Ava murmured. Tangling limbs with him, she threaded her fingers through his dark hair, noting there wasn't as much of it as the last time she'd run fingers through it. "Why'd you cut your hair? I liked it long."

His chest vibrated under her cheek. "Part of my new image."

"You don't need a new image. I liked you the way you were."

"Even perfection can be improved."

She slapped his chest. "Fine. I'll cut my hair too, then."

That got a reaction. "I suggest you wouldn't dare." He pulled her head up gently by said hair, winding it around his fingers and bringing it to his nose for a whiff. "Long as a Martian winter," he murmured.

Ava laughed. "I guess my space cooties did you some good, after all."

"If it wasn't for you and your nosy questions, I'd have never learned the truth."

"I'm sorry it happened at such a lousy time."

"There's a good time?"

"I felt somewhat responsible for your distress."

Arnie growled deep in his chest. "Although I suggest I like your being responsible for me, don't be on that particular score. My family was right to conclude I'm missing a few marbles. I can't believe I never noticed something was wrong with the family portrait."

Ava tugged his head down for a soul-sucking kiss. "I like it that you don't pay attention to external trappings."

He captured her lip in his teeth, gave it a nibble then pulled back to run a wolfish gaze up and down her body. "I noticed yours, and those trappings trapped me but good."

"I'm so happy," she sighed.

"I'm happy too. Happier than I've ever been."

"So when are you going to call your birth parents?"

He let silence stretch between them while Ava listened to the comforting sounds of his heartbeat, the steady intake of breath, the life sounds of a soul so precious she couldn't think of him without choking up.

"According to my goofball brother, I'd have to wait light-years to hear back from them. He thinks I came from outer space."

She listened as he outlined Tiny's findings. So this is what he'd left out of the initial version. Understandable.

The facts alerted every system in her body.

The alien theme had streaked through their relationship from the beginning and simply wouldn't slow down. First Arnie had believed she was an alien, then she had thoughts of him being one, then The Others, the voices, the visions of flying, the comet and that *smell*…

Could that've been an apparition of Arnie's mother ship? Had it crashed, thus instilling in him the unlikely fear of flying?

*Michael.* Why did that name slap her into déjà vu?

Arnie appeared from nowhere. Had no history. Possessed extreme intelligence. Could read minds when he wanted to. And those eyes…

Michael! The being called Anthros had said *Michael's* destiny depended on her. Had he really meant *Arnie's* destiny depended on her?

The odd feelings that'd fluttered in her stomach all along merged with everything she knew from her studies in astrobiology then knotted with Tiny's theory into one giant, immutable Truth. "Arnie." She licked suddenly dry lips as a swollen wave of unprecedented, chill-inducing delight swept through her. "What if Robert Walker isn't your natural father? What if Tiny's assumptions are correct?" Beneath her, he stiffened. "Let's pretend they are, for a minute."

"Sure. Except I suggest you're not pretending."

She hiked herself up on an elbow and looked into his face. "What if I'm not?"

He stared back at her. "Well, I suggest that's a funny thing." He swiped at his mouth, as if trying to wipe away his next words.

"Why?"

"Because I'm not sure I can totally put your mind to rest about it, either."

She grabbed his hand and wove their fingers together, excitement tightening around her chest until she had to force the words out. "What do you mean?" If they were both thinking the same thing, the entire scientific universe was about to tilt.

"One reason it took me a week to come and get you was because I had some DNA tests done. I wanted to get the last word on whether I was a freakin' human or a freakin' freak."

"And?" Did she shriek the word?

"The upshot is, I appear human. But there's a deviation the geeks are scratching their heads over. They said it's consistent with extreme radiation exposure. Like something they'd expect to see in a Hiroshima survivor. Except I was never anywhere close to that much radiation. Unless Tiny is to be believed."

Her billowed sails flapped a little. "Well, maybe you weren't exposed. Maybe it's a protective gene mutation, one for living in an area of high radiation. You don't have to have necessarily been exposed to something to have a mutation. You might have inherited it."

"The geeks mentioned that. Unfortunately, I'd have to have a family history to find out."

"Or have a child," she said automatically.

They stared at each other. He reached out and ran a light hand over her head and down her neck. Then he shrugged his eyebrows, blinked and looked away in a curiously guarded manner. "I suggest you might want to think long and hard about mating with me."

Her heart sputtered and seized. He'd had a battery of tests all alone with no one to hold his hand, and had come all this way to get her only to have to risk it all with that one, simple statement. "If it's inheritable, it hasn't hurt you." Her mind raced furiously. His DNA was human except for one known mutation. That meant they could have "normal" children no matter what else he turned out to be. Not that it made any difference to her. In fact, rather than feeling frightened, as she supposed a sane person might feel, she was elated. Excited. Exhilarated. She'd waited and hoped a lifetime for this.

"Yet," he added softly.

"Oh Arnie. People get married and have children all the time without genetic testing. It's a leap of faith. A leap of love! Would you not marry me even if we knew for sure I had some time bomb ticking in my body?"

"I'd marry you no matter what."

"Same for me. We're in this together. We can do more research, have more tests if you want, but there's no way I'm not mating with you. For life."

"Even if I'm a different life form?"

"Especially if you're a different life form." She paused and processed his statement. Coming from his current emotional climate, it was as near an acknowledgement of his heritage as she was likely to get anytime soon. She decided to press further, encourage him to tease out his true feelings. "Then you believe you *did* come to Earth on Apollo Thirteen?"

"Well, it's certainly worth investigating. I don't know if we can ever prove it. But there is that photograph, and it makes sense in a twisted way."

Yeah. It did. "How do you feel about it?"

"The same way I felt when I heard I wasn't really a Simpson. There's no difference, really." He held out his hands as if weighing two things for comparison. "Not a Simpson, not a human being." He barked out a laugh. "It's not the worst thing in the world, although someday I'd like to find out exactly what I am."

"Yeah. Me too."

He grinned. "In a weird way, I'm excited about it. Hell, I've lived a good life this long not knowing about it, so nothing has changed except my own awareness." He paused and drew in a breath. "What about you? How do you feel about it?"

"More in love than I ever thought possible." But she had a lot of questions. Like, where did she fit into this puzzle? Why could she telecommunicate with him so effortlessly? Was she his Earthling familiar? Or had she been brought here too as part of some master design?

Robert Walker had to be contacted. Soon.

"Anyway, if Robert Walker was an engineer for the space program...well...I figure if he reckoned I helped save the astronauts, maybe I did. It's a stretch. But it's given me a reason to have more faith in myself."

So Arnie's missing pieces had finally settled into place, she thought. He'd been paralyzed with doubt all these years. Never knowing who he was, or where he fit in had subconsciously undermined his confidence and propelled him along an easier path than he might otherwise have chosen.

Is that what had happened to her father? Had his fears had kept him from living up to his potential? Had they crippled him?

He'd encouraged her to live up to hers. He'd had the strength for that. And more than any money he might've left for her and her mother had he worked harder, that was his greatest legacy.

At long last, it seemed enough. Perhaps that'd been his purpose. And he'd fulfilled it.

She couldn't argue against it anymore. Couldn't ask for more.

They hugged tightly. Ava sucked in Arnie's scent, lapped up his flavor and reveled in the glory of ownership. He had his fears and insecurities just like everyone else, despite the magnitude of his brain capacity. The difference with Arnie was that he found a way to overcome them.

"Being abducted might be the best thing that ever happened to you," she joked.

"Nah," he said. "You're the best thing that ever happened to me. Getting stolen as a child is just the icing."

They snickered.

"I wonder what'll happen next," Arnie mused. "This has been one hairy week."

"That's an understatement." Never in her life had she imagined falling in love with E.T. Yet, it seemed natural. As if it'd been her fate all along.

However, they still had one last row to hoe. Time to tell him she was selling her practice. Swallowing her fear of the many unknowns to come, she burrowed her face in his neck and said, "I'm moving to Flintlock."

Silence.

She cracked an eye and peered up at him. "Well?"

He was looking at her like she'd gone loony. "Why would you want to do that?"

"Because you're there."

"You're all wrong for that dump. Even I can see that."

"But, Arnie." Her eyes filled. "I'd die without you."

"Who said you had to live without me?" He chucked her chin with his knuckles and searched her face with his eyes.

"I couldn't take you away from Flintlock, not now, after all that happened." She couldn't take her eyes off his. They'd softened and grown large and were filling once again with the brimstone swirls that hypnotized her.

"What about your job?" he asked softly.

"I'll start a new practice."

His eyes hardened again, briefly. "On who, Tiny, Marty and Ray? I suggest not."

Against the odds, his protestations were lifting her heart out of the gloom and into the realm of hope for the first time since she'd met him. Could he possibly want to live here? Could Lorna have been wrong all along?

"What do you suggest, then?" she whispered, hardly daring for this one wish to be granted.

"That we stay right here."

There it was. Genius Chrysler! She flopped down on his chest, cracked a smile that grew to a grin that emerged as a chuckle until soon, she was laughing in hysterical release, moisture streaming from every facial orifice.

"What's so funny?" he asked, making her laugh even harder. He swiped his wet chest and peered at his hand. "Okay, I'm calling 911."

"Wait," she gasped. "Arnie. All this time I thought you wanted to stay in Flintlock. Lorna said you loved it there."

He shrugged. "I did. Except after you left, it developed all the attractive qualities of an unwashed armpit."

"But your family."

"I'll buy an airplane, fly out twice a month—"

"You'll *fly*?"

"I flew out here to get you."

Yes, he did—another fear he'd found the strength to overcome. For her. A gush of pure love melted her limbs and she puddled against him. "I wish I could buy one for you. But if you're only going to be working part-time in Flintlock…"

He sat her upright, fluffing a pillow and wedging it behind her back then he perched on the edge of the mattress beside her, stroking her leg. "I figure on working a few years and when you start popping babies, I'll be a househusband."

She blinked. "A househusband?"

He squeezed her ankle. "You see enough poop in a day. You won't want to be changing diapers."

Ava's head started spinning. Was this guy for real? She would get to go off to work in the morning, come home to a clean house and a cooked dinner, play with her baby, put it to bed then play with her husband? Was this Minneapolis, or heaven?

But he still needed to realize he wouldn't get to see his family twice a month. "I hate to bust your bubble, but even with my substantial salary, I doubt we can buy a plane. I'm still paying off loans."

Arnie's infamous sly grin inched across his face. "Oh yeah." He slapped his forehead. "I forgot to tell you."

"Forgot to tell me what?" she intoned.

"Remember that friend of Mr. Merryfield's?"

Ava's heart seized. "Yes."

"Turns out he needed a consultant with just my qualifications."

"And?"

Arnie scratched his chin, appraising her through half-closed lids, drawing out the torture. "I can telecommute whenever I want and the job pays pretty well."

"Arnie! How much, dammit!"

He laughed, a triumphant, rich, masculine laugh. "Only about ten thousand dollars a minute."

"What?" she shrieked.

He back-pedaled. "I suggest that's a bit of an exaggeration. We're still negotiating. But trust me on this." He leaned forward and kissed her. "The signing bonus is a sweet six figures. Hurt for money we will not."

Ava threw her arms around him for a bigger wetter smooch. "When do we get married?"

He grinned. "Oh sure, now that I'm a millionaire executive, you can't wait to marry me."

She smacked his arm. "So I have bad timing. Shoot me."

He spread her out and crawled on top of her, gyrating gently until they fit snuggly together. "For someone who doesn't believe in it, you have beautiful timing. You also have a beautiful body and a beautiful mind." Pulling back a few inches and absorbing her with his eyes, he shook his head. "I suggest you are simply out of this world."

"I counter-suggest," she said on a blissful sigh. "*You* are the one who's out of this world."

# CPILOGUC

Arnie sat on the sofa, the volume of the TV science channel turned low, watching dinosaurs roam the Earth and his baby son twitch in sleep.

Michael lay on his lap, sucking his fist while his tiny eyes rolled in REM sleep. What could this newborn creature be dreaming about? Probably dark wet tunnels, a squeegee effect on his head, agonized screams and sudden blinding light.

Nice way to start life. No wonder people were screwed up.

Ava materialized from the shower, all dressed up, bustling around the kitchen. Arnie frowned, checking the time and date on TV. Usually Sundays were lazy days.

"What's up?" he asked, scooping Michael into the hollow of his arm and rising to join her.

She brushed a dry kiss against his cheek. Despite giving birth only three months ago, her waist had shrunk back to normal leaving behind a soft little pooch along her abdomen he loved to squish his face into.

"I forgot to tell you?"

Her voice sounded brittle and bright. *Faker*. "Tell me what?"

She waved a burnt potholder in his direction. "We're having company for lunch. I invited this new couple over."

"New couple?"

Ava stumbled over her words. Odd behavior indeed. "This couple I met," she said vaguely.

Arnie raised his eyebrows, but she turned away as if she didn't see. He decided to let it drop. She was distracted by the roast beef in the oven and it wasn't all that unusual for them to entertain. Just not normal for a Sunday afternoon.

"Should I get dressed?" he asked, peering down at his customary costume — jeans and an AirGage T-shirt.

"What? Oh. Yes. Wear something nice, sweetie." She smiled at Michael, pressed a kiss on his head and turned back to the peas.

Arnie set the infant in his bassinet and ambled down the hall. These past eighteen months married to Ava, feeling his child grow inside her, learning her inside out had been the highlight of his life.

He couldn't believe one man could have all this luck. Their bank account swelled on a daily basis from his consulting job, his Mooney waited at the airport, his relationship with his adopted family grew stronger by the minute. He had the best of both worlds. All worlds, he chuckled, casting an eye down the hallway at *The Being*.

And her profession had stopped bothering him. Mostly. She came home every night with hilarious stories, full of energy and appreciation for what he did during the day. Sure as shooting stars, he felt fulfilled in every way. Save one.

After undergoing extensive genetic testing, the conclusions he and his friends had been forced to draw indicated that at best he was an excruciatingly peculiar human. More likely, however, he was from a heretofore unknown bloodline. And Michael had inherited his mutations.

Under cloak of extreme secrecy, they were conducting further tests and comparing them more closely with the DNA database as it continued to grow across the planet.

One of these days he would find out with unflinching certainty where he came from and who his original parents were. He already figured his roots had some connection with the Observers because their chatter had become almost unbearable. They seemed to want something from him. Ava thought they wanted him to open his mind to communicate. But so far he'd been unable to make himself and he pretty much knew why—they would answer all his questions.

Yeah. He and denial had been best pals for too long.

Paying careful attention to his morning stubble, Arnie finished shaving and checked himself out just as the doorbell rang.

"I'll get it," Ava sang.

Arnie quickly tucked his olive green oxford shirt into his khakis, tightened his belt and adjusted his tie.

Soft voices from the living room reached his ears. Sounded like a pretty young couple, so he was surprised when he strode down the hall and spotted a small man with steel gray hair. He wore a dark, elegantly cut suit with a starched white shirt. Arnie recognized the quality now that he'd been out in the workforce so long.

For a moment, Ava's tall frame hid the woman then she stepped aside, turning to Arnie with a beaming smile.

The woman saw him and gasped, hand flying to her breast. The man braced her back with his arm when it looked as if she might swoon.

Arnie registered the man's quiet distress then transferred his gaze to the woman's face.

His mouth dried up. Even though her features were contorted with shock and emotion, he recognized her right off the bat.

From her photograph on the E.T.I. website.

She was the founder and CEO. What was she doing here? A creeping vine wrapped around his backbone as her dark eyes turned silver. She had mood eyes too. Yet she looked nothing like him. She couldn't be his real mother. Could she? He tried to prepare himself for the denouement.

From a faraway place he heard Ava say, "Robert and Marjorie Walker, meet Arnold Marr Simpson."

"Are you my biological parents?" he blurted. Seemed the little wifey had decided to press the issue. Okay. He could deal with it. He wasn't angry. She was right. It was time.

Robert Walker squared his shoulders and gave his tie a miniscule adjustment. "Not exactly," he said, advancing with a dazzling smile, an extended hand and a bright, tear-filled gaze. "But I suggest I might know where you can find them."

\* \* \* \* \*

**Memorandum: Urgent!**

**Star Date: 10,050**

**From: Queen Win**

**To: InterGalactic Control Center**

Probabilist Anthros has vanished after allowing our plant to mate with a human! He is a traitor and should be considered armed and dangerous.

Who knows what the hybrid babe will turn out to be, which forces will dominate or what havoc it will wreak on the universe?

The child is to be watched closely and monitored.

Our future depends on it.

*And bring me Anthros' head on a plate!*

*Enjoy An Excerpt From:*

# RIDING RANGER

*Copyright © CIANA STONE, 2006.*

*All Rights Reserved, Ellora's Cave, Inc.*

Hi, John,

Right now you're asking yourself how I managed to get into your apartment without being detected. In case you haven't been paying close attention, let me clarify. Just like you, I am good at what I do and getting into your apartment really wasn't much challenge at all.

I have to say that your choice of evening attire was very stimulating. Those low-slung pj bottoms cling nicely and reveal just enough to make the imagination run wild. Of course, you may want to rethink the plaid.

But discussing your fashion sense is not why I dropped this off for you. I want to make you an offer. A one-time, take it or leave it, offer. Close the case on the Lone Ranger and then let's you and I meet in person and discuss where we go from there.

I know I intrigue you, John. And I know that despite not knowing exactly how I look, you want me. Your…condition while you were reading my journal stands as testament to that.

Now don't be embarrassed. I'm flattered. And more than that, I'm just as turned on by you. Why, just this evening I was imagining what it would be like if we got together. Shall I tell you how I imagine it?

It's late. Your apartment is dark, with only the lights of the city filtering in through the blinds. You're lying on the couch in those yummy worn jeans you're fond of wearing, the ones with the hole in the left knee.

I drop in on the balcony and slide open the door. You see my shadow—just a shadowy dark form against the dim light. Immediately you reach for your weapon. Unlike many times when you leave it on your bedroom dresser, this night it's on the coffee table in front of you. You pull it free from its holster as I part the blinds and cross the threshold.

"Freeze," you order in your best bureau voice. "Hands where I can see them."

"Whatever you say," I respond and spread my arms out wide to my sides.

You rise from the couch and approach me warily. As you draw close the fine shafts of light penetrating the spaces in the blinds fall across you. I can see the set of your jaw, the intensity in your eyes. The tension in the muscles of your arms and torso.

You stop in front of me, your gun leveled at my head and I smile. "Hello, John," I say.

"Who are you?" you ask, even though I suspect you know the answer.

"It's me, John. I'm here, just like I promised."

Your eyes give you away, your surprise that I'm really there in the flesh, your suspicion that I'm not who you think, but someone who is playing with you, and your excitement that maybe this is indeed real.

Your eyes rake over me, from the top of my black ski-masked head, down the lines of my black Lycra-encased body to the soles of my black shoes. One quick pass before your eyes return to lock with mine.

"Are you going to shoot me, John?" I ask and step closer, into the fall of light so that my eyes are revealed to you.

You step back from me, demonstrating your mistrust and wariness and for a few long moments we simply stare at one another. "How do I know it's you?" you ask in a harsh whisper.

"You know, John," I reply. "Who else would…drop in on you this way? Who else has occupied your mind and interrupted your sleep for the last year? What would you have me do to prove myself to you? Shall I remind you of my first little caper? Would you like to meet Buffy? Shall I reveal myself to you at last, John?"

"Yes," you say in a voice that is tight with tension and mounting excitement.

"Have a seat," I suggest. "And turn on a light, John."

You back over to the couch and take a seat then fumble for the light on the end table. Dim light brightens the room.

I move my arms from their widespread position to reach up and pull the ski mask from my head. My hair spills free. Your eyes widen in surprise. I'm not what you expected, not what any of them suspected. But it's obvious that you like what you see so I smile and drop the mask.

Your eyes follow the movement of my hands as I slowly unzip the tight bodysuit from neck to groin. With slow seductive movements, I wiggle the top half from my body. My nipples pucker at the cool air from the overhead ceiling fan.

I turn so that my back is to you and work the tight material down over my hips.

~ ~ ~ ~ ~

John's cock jumped to life as he read her words and his balls ached. The woman was determined to kill him. With a curse, he stripped off his pants…

# Why an electronic book?

We live in the Information Age—an exciting time in the history of human civilization, in which technology rules supreme and continues to progress in leaps and bounds every minute of every day. For a multitude of reasons, more and more avid literary fans are opting to purchase e-books instead of paper books. The question from those not yet initiated into the world of electronic reading is simply: *Why?*

1. ***Price.*** An electronic title at Ellora's Cave Publishing and Cerridwen Press runs anywhere from 40% to 75% less than the cover price of the exact same title in paperback format. Why? Basic mathematics and cost. It is less expensive to publish an e-book (no paper and printing, no warehousing and shipping) than it is to publish a paperback, so the savings are passed along to the consumer.

2. ***Space.*** Running out of room in your house for your books? That is one worry you will never have with electronic books. For a low one-time cost, you can purchase a handheld device specifically designed for e-reading. Many e-readers have large, convenient screens for viewing. Better yet, hundreds of titles can be stored within your new library—on a single microchip. There are a variety of e-readers from different manufacturers. You can also read e-books on your PC or laptop computer. (Please note that Ellora's

Cave does not endorse any specific brands. You can check our websites at www.ellorascave.com or www.cerridwenpress.com for information we make available to new consumers.)

3. *Mobility.* Because your new e-library consists of only a microchip within a small, easily transportable e-reader, your entire cache of books can be taken with you wherever you go.

4. *Personal Viewing Preferences.* Are the words you are currently reading too small? Too large? Too… ANNOYING? Paperback books cannot be modified according to personal preferences, but e-books can.

5. *Instant Gratification.* Is it the middle of the night and all the bookstores near you are closed? Are you tired of waiting days, sometimes weeks, for bookstores to ship the novels you bought? Ellora's Cave Publishing sells instantaneous downloads twenty-four hours a day, seven days a week, every day of the year. Our webstore is never closed. Our e-book delivery system is 100% automated, meaning your order is filled as soon as you pay for it.

Those are a few of the top reasons why electronic books are replacing paperbacks for many avid readers.

As always, Ellora's Cave and Cerridwen Press welcome your questions and comments. We invite you to email us at Comments@ellorascave.com or write to us directly at Ellora's Cave Publishing Inc., 1056 Home Avenue, Akron, OH 44310-3502.

# THE
# ⚲ ELLORA'S CAVE ⚲
# LIBRARY

Stay up to date with Ellora's Cave Titles in
Print with our Quarterly Catalog.

TO RECIEVE A CATALOG,
SEND AN EMAIL WITH YOUR NAME
AND MAILING ADDRESS TO:


## CATALOG@ELLORASCAVE.COM
OR SEND A LETTER OR POSTCARD
WITH YOUR MAILING ADDRESS TO:


CATALOG REQUEST
c/o ELLORA'S CAVE PUBLISHING, INC.
1056 HOME AVENUE
AKRON, OHIO 44310-3502

erridwen, the Celtic Goddess of wisdom, was the muse who brought inspiration to storytellers and those in the creative arts. Cerridwen Press encompasses the best and most innovative stories in all genres of today's fiction. Visit our site and discover the newest titles by talented authors who still get inspired - much like the ancient storytellers did, once upon a time.

## Cerridwen Press

www.cerridwenpress.com

# Cerrídwen Press

## Monthly Newsletter

News
Author Appearances
Book Signings
New Releases
Contests
Author Profiles
Feature Articles

Available online at
www.CerridwenPress.com

*Discover for yourself why readers can't get enough of the multiple award-winning publisher*

*Ellora's Cave.*

*Whether you prefer e-books or paperbacks,*

*be sure to visit EC on the web at*
*www.ellorascave.com*

*for an erotic reading experience that will leave you breathless.*